True Love with a Bad Boy

A novella By Nakiala Comeaux

Thank you for purchasing, "True Love with A Bad Boy." Feel free to browse Amazon for the rest of my catalog. I hope you enjoy and thank you for the support. Below is a list of my previous work and social media contact.

- Forever my Savage: A Yungin and His Lady 1-4

- Daughter of a Trap King 1-4
- I Love you For My Soul
- She was a Savage, He was the realist
- My Louisiana Thug 1-3
- The First 48: Money Making Meeka 1 -3
- Thankful for my Real Hitta (An Anthology)
- Hood Love and Haunted Nights (An Anthology)
- Thuggin Around the Christmas Tree (An Anthology)
- No Matter What, I Choose You 1 and 2 Finale
- Married to a New York Menace 1 and 2 Finale
- "Trap Kings and the Women Who Love Them 1 and 2 Finale
- Ain't No Love In Hip Hop: Love vs Fame 1 and 2 Finale

Facebook Page: Ravonne Ramar

Facebook Like Page: Author Ravonne Ramar

Facebook Reading Group: Author Ravonne Ramar's Reading Group

Snapchat: Authorki16

Instagram: _authorravonne_

"Brody, Brody, Brody, my sweet Brody. Never in a million years I thought our lives would be like this, but I'm down to ride to the very end. I love you with all my heart, remember that." ~Kamren Cotton, wife of Brody Cotton the 3rd.

Chapter 1 (January 2012)

"Man, it's fuckin' cold, bruh," Savage rubbed his hands together, saying. The heater was pumping, but it felt like his body wasn't warm enough.

"Who you telling? I didn't think it could get this cold in the dirty south," Brody chuckled, with a smirk on his face.

Sitting quietly in the back seat of the black 2010 Yukon, Brody tried to ease his mind before shit popped off. Since the windows were illegally tinted, he didn't mind that his Glock 17 sat on his lap. On top of that, it was midnight and the streets were pitch black clear of cars and people. A few days ago, Opelousas experience what the city would call a snow day, so everything was tucked in the houses at midnight. Well, everyone who wasn't up to no-good was tucked tightly in the house. Ice mostly covered the ground, but it gave everyone a reason to cancel school and work. The roads were still icy, but that didn't stop Brody, Savage, Big Head, and True Love, from being the true criminals they were at heart.

Two weeks ago, someone robbed Savage's home out of $2,000 and six guns. Luckily, he was out of town, and didn't get hurt, but to him, that wasn't a loss. Word got back to him who did the robbery and where they trapped out. Tonight, they were clearing the business, and didn't care who got hurt in the process. Savage wasn't worrying about retrieving the money or guns, he only wanted revenge and to prove a point. Never cross him, or take what wasn't yours, especially from a nigga like him, who didn't have any sense. Everyone knew Savage as a hot head, who lived for this kind of shit. It was only a matter of time he crossed paths with his next victim. Besides, he didn't mind adding another body to his hit list.

"Say, B, is there still any food left over? That okra was the truth. Kamren gives my mama a run for her money," Savage rubbed his six pack abs, laughing. Savage tried to avoid the street life, but it basically sucked him in. He always said the street life chose him and he didn't choose it.

At the age of ten, Savage's mother was involved in a terrible accident. It left her paralyzed from the hip down. With a father in prison sentenced to life for murder, he only had the streets to turn to.

Sucking him in with open arms, Savage always felt like the trenches only loved him.

"I think so, that's if she didn't take any to work. You know she likes to feed all the nurses on her floor." Brody laughed. Twenty-six years old Brody Samuel Cotton the 3rd, the quiet one of the crew. He never said much, he liked his actions to speak for him, because they always said how he truly felt. Brody had everyone fooled with his baby face and curly air-fro. If you took one look at him, you only saw a sweet boy, with clear beige skin. Once you got to know him, that thought faded away in seconds. In the streets, Brody was labeled as a no good muthafucka, which he took pride in. His reputation and street credentials didn't happen overnight. It took years of pull ups, shoot outs, and jacking, to gain the reputation he did.

"I sure hope she didn't feed them bitches today, I'm starving." Savage laughed.

"Food should be the last thing on your mind." Big Head mumbled, loudly, that was the way he spoke.

"Nigga, mind your business, I'm talking to B." Savage laughed.

Brody shook his head, chuckling at his friend's petty argument. Instead of chiming in, Brody loaded his gun, while staring at the wallpaper on his phone. It was a picture of his twenty- five-year-old girlfriend, Kamren Evans. Kamren and Brody had been dating for six years, she probably was the best thing that happened to him. If you asked Brody about Kamren, she was the ground he walked on. Kam was the reason the sun shined so brightly and the reason the sun set perfectly when it did. She also was the reason he stayed out of prison and the graveyard. That was Kamren's two missions with Brody, she made sure she fulfilled them every day.

"These niggas better throw their hands high in the air. I don't care who's about to hit Booray. I'm tired and I don't feel like hearing no grown ass man beg for nothing. POW! POW! POW! I want every nigga in there to make their pockets look like bunny ears." True Love laughed, dapping Savage, who was tickled by what

True Love worded. He pointed his iron towards the window, pretending to shoot. One thing about True Love, he had a good aim, and was always shooting to kill. He never wasted bullets to prove a point or scare a nigga.

"Fuckin' right, I don't have time for the extra shit tonight. All that crying and begging for your life when you're getting robbed, is getting old. On top of that, I have to be home by 2:30 am, you know Rachel gets off at 3:00 am. If I'm not home, tucked in bed, when she gets there, she will beat my ass like a true savage. You should call her Savage, instead of me." Savage laughed.

"Savage, I have questions and I need answers." Big Head said.

"What's up, fool?"

"What kind of criminal are you? You're about to do a stick up, but you have a curfew? I guess pussy really do rule the world," Big Head said, making Savage shrug his broad shoulders, laughing. True Love always teased Savage about his shoulders that reminded him of a coat hanger. He always laughed and brushed it off, but deep down inside, he didn't think it was funny. As a kid, Savage was teased about his shoulders, and always found himself in fights because of his flaw. He didn't care how big, mean, or tall, you were, Savage didn't mind putting you on your pockets for teasing him. That's how he got the nickname Savage. Once he got that nickname, Savage's behavior got out of hand and no one could handle him.

"Man, call it what you want, I love my girl more than I love these niggas. I'm not trying to lose her behind this."

"Savage and Brody are the softest criminals I know! My nigga, I know a lot of criminals, that should tell you a lot," True Love turned around, staring at Brody.

"Huh?" Brody seemed lost and a little confused, when True Love called his name. Somehow, he tuned out the entire conversation, while staring at the picture. Big Head noticed what Brody was staring at and he grabbed his phone. Brody attempted to snatch the phone back, but he was too slow.

"My point exactly," Big Head showed everyone the picture, laughing. Then he tossed the phone back to Brody, still laughing.

"So, what? I love my girl. I'll stand at the top of Mount Everest to shout it. Maybe if Big Head and True Love showed some emotions, they could find love. These streets don't love you, clowns, but I thought y'all knew that."

"PREACH, my brother, PREACH! Love is good for the soul, just like soul food." Savage laughed. Savage was twenty years old, but his age didn't mean anything. By the age of seventeen, he made a very notorious name for himself. Everyone knew him as the Wayne "Silk" Perry, of the Dirty South. His murder game was sick, his tear drops under his right eye proved it. He spent majority of his childhood in and out of detention centers, because he didn't give a fuck about the way he lived his young life.

Brandon Barre, aka Savage, is originally from Eunice, Louisiana. His family moved to Opelousas when he was sixteen. Rumor has it that Savage killed 32-year-old Eli Frances the first night his family moved to Opelousas. Supposedly, Eli tried to rob Savage, but things turned ugly. Besides Savage and Eli, I guess the world will never know what really happened.

"Big Head, do you hear these clowns?!" True Love asked.

"Yea, I hear this, but I wish I didn't. They sound like two clowns, just call them Willie FuFu and Willie Lump Lump."

"Hell yea, comparing pussy ass love to food. Man, these niggas are tripping, they should be put in a straightjacket." He laughed.

"Love is good, but have you ever had chicken wings from The Back? Now that's love right there, homie," Big Head rubbed his big belly, making everyone laugh.

"Of course, his fat ass would choose food over love. Enough about that, it's time to do this and get it over with." As Big Head approached the Compress Road, he turned the SUV's lights off. He then reached under the seatt for the black ski mask placing it right above his forehead.

"Look, we have two minutes to do this. Actually, we have three minutes tops, to get in and get out. No extra shit, especially you, Savage! We don't have time for you to go through anybody's pockets," Big Head used his gun to point at Savage.

"I hear you, damn." Savage said, pulling his ski mask over his face and grabbing his gun. Tucking his nine-millimeter under his shirt, Savage hoped out of the Yukon, ready to clear the business. Everyone else slowly got out of the Yukon, creeping through the dark neighborhood. The area was quiet, they couldn't make much noise if they weren't trying to leave a trace behind.

With wide stretched eyes, Big Head scanned the three brick houses, making sure no one was around. Then he pointed at the tan and royal blue house, making an evil grin appear on Savage's face. He couldn't wait to kick the door in, leaving his size ten Timberland footprint. His motto was, "Catch a body a day and you'll keep the fuck niggas away."

"Y'all ready?" Big head looked at everyone and they shook their heads. Savage took a step back, ramming his size nine boots into the front door. Two women shouted at the top of their lungs, who were on the floor naked sitting Indian style. Savage wanted to laugh, but he knew it would only piss Big Head off.

A variety of pills and sandwich bags surrounded the women. Smaller bags of cocaine sat between one of the women's leg. True Love kicked the bags over, powder, and the tip of his shoe, slammed the girl's chin. Blood started to drip from her face and she cried. True Love laughed, he wasn't bothered, at all.

"AAAHHHHHHHHHHHH, oh no." The second woman screamed louder, using her hands to cover her breasts.

The other woman tried to crawl away, but True Love snatched her hair. Her wig slipped off and her miniature ponytail was exposed. True Love grabbed her little ponytail and handled her like a doll. From the moment he walked through the door, he knew who she was. He's been waiting to get his hand on Ka' Meka Lees and he finally got his opportunity. Six months ago, Ka' Meka wrote a false statement on him to help her best friend. That could explain why True Love doesn't trust anyone.

"EVERYBODY, GET THE FUCK DOWN," Big Head shouted, and waved the gun at everyone. Everyone froze and tossed their hands in the air. Ka' Meka tried to toss her hands in the air, but True Love pulled her ponytail tighter.

"You, niggas, know what time it is! Get the fuck on the floor and this shit will go smooth. Just a bullet to the head, that's all," Savage approached one of the guys. With a terrified look on his face, the guy back peddled, attempting to find safety. Savage put the barrel of the gun into the guy's mouth and **BOOM!**

Ka'meka screamed and closed her eyes. Blood and brain mattered splashed all over Savage, but he didn't care. Hearing a head explode, was like music to his ears. Everyone chose a body and began shooting. Before you knew it, the cleaned living room turned into a pool of blood, body parts were everywhere.

"Two minutes is up, let's go." Brody shouted and ran to the door. Everyone followed behind Brody and ran to the Yukon. Since Big Head left the truck running, they hoped in and he sped off.

"Damn, that was fun," True Love pulled the ski-mask off his face reaching for the empty duffle bag to place it in.

"I wouldn't call it fun, but do you," Brody wiped his sweaty face with his sleeve and pulled the black sweater off his body. The ski mask was wrapped in the sweater and he tossed it into the bag. Savage controlled the steering wheel while Big Head removed the ski mask and sweater from his body. Once he was done, he tossed the clothes to Savage. Savage removed the clothing, handing everything to True Love. He then zipped the duffle bag pointing to the field to the left. Big Head nodded his head pulling over.

"Savage, hand me the matches and lighter." Savage handed him the lighter and matches. True Love jumped out of the Yukon and quickly lit the bag on fire. Within seconds, the bag was in flames. True Love rushed to get back in the Yukon and Big Head sped off.

"Another mission completed." True Love said.

"Just like the rest of them, another cold case." Brody laughed.

"We're going to ride to Baton Rouge and turn right back around." Big Head said.

Within an hour, everyone's phone was ringing. Some people's phones rang more than others. Like Savage and Brody, to be specific. Kamren called Brody's phone non-stop, but he didn't answer it. He knew he had a lot of explaining to do once he got home. Especially how he left home in a complete different set of clothes. Kamren wasn't going to be okay with a random story Brody would make. He had to have a legit story, and a few back up stories, just in case she didn't believe one.

Once they made it back in town, the city's streets were flooded with cops. They knew the investigation had started.

"I swear, I hate this messy ass town. News spread like wildfire." Savage said, as he yawned.

"More like AIDS, yea. I bet they have twenty stories already." True Love said, and shook his head.

"I know, I hope Kamren wasn't calling because of that." Brody said.

"Don't be stupid, B, you know that's why she was calling." Big Head said.

"That's why I'm going to play retarded when I get home." He laughed.

"Short bus shawty retarded?" Big Head asked.

"Short bus shawty, 225 retarded. I don't know anything, I didn't see anything, and I damn sure didn't do anything." Brody said, tossing his hands into the hair.

"I know that's why my girl was calling, but I'm going to lie and tell her I was sleeping."

"This clown literally, blew a man's head off his shoulders. Now, he's going to lie and tell his girl he was sleepin'." Big Head said and laughed.

"Like I said earlier, I'm trying to keep my woman. Fuck you, niggas," he smiled and pulled his phone out. Big Head slowly turned onto Brody's street, making Brody's heart drop. He could see Kamren's white 2011 Malibu parked in the driveway. He knew she had to be home waiting for him to step foot into the door.

Damn it, he said to himself.

"Hit me up in the morning, B," True Love dapped Brody as he got out of the Yukon. Big Head blew the horn and drove off. Brody looked over his shoulder and smacked his lips. He knew he blew the horn purposely.

"Please be sleeping, please be sleeping." Brody whispered to himself. He pulled his house key out of his pocket and slowly walked into the dark house. Since all the lights were off, he figured Kamren had to be sleeping. The door squeaked, his heart dropped. Once the door closed he exhaled.

"Brody Samuel Cotton the fuckingThird."

"Kamren Olese Evans, but soon to be Cotton, what's up, baby?"

"Where were you?" Standing at the top of the staircase, Kamren's flat tone made Brody nervous. When Kam was too calm like this, Brody knew shit could only get ugly between them.

He turned the living room light on and squinted his eyes to get a better view of Kamren. Her soft hair was in a low ponytail, just like Brody liked it. Even though he could sense her attitude, she still looked cute in her purple sports bra and his black Haynes boxers.

"I told you I was with True Love, Big Head, and Savage."

"Hhmm, such a HORRIBLE, combination. I just got a phone call that there was a shooting on the Compress Road. Do you know anything about it, Brody?"

"Baby, I didn't have anything to do with that," Brody tossed his hoodie on the chair and approached the staircase. She shook her head and extended her short arm out.

"Don't lie to me and don't even think about taking a step on these stairs. It's crazy how this is the second shooting this month and you weren't home. Stay your ass on the couch tonight, ole lying ass. I'm too heated to finish this conversation with you."

"Come on baby, you're tripping." Brody said.

"No, I'm not, but you're lying in my face Brody. The last shooting, we did this same little two step. You lie for hours, you made up an entire story about where you were. I didn't believe any of it from jump, then you finally confessed." With an attitude, Kamren slowly walked down the stairs and stood in the middle.

"Kamren, can we please talk about this in the morning? I'm lowkey tired and hungry," Brody's stomach was growling, plus, he was struggling to keep his slanted eyes open. He wanted to end the conversation, by running up the stairs, but that would only start another argument.

"When will you get it together, Brody? You can't live this life forever, I won't stay with you if you think dumb shit. You promised me you were going back to school and find a job. You'll say anything while we're fucking and I'm so stupid to believe it. Good night, Brody." Rolling her eyes, Kamren charged upstairs, leaving Brody alone in his thoughts. Brody exhaled quietly following behind her, but also regretting some of the thigs he said. Once she noticed Brody was following behind her, she rushed into the bedroom. Kamren tried to close the door, but Brody ran into the room in just enough time.

"Baby, you know that's not the case, don't say that. You shouldn't think like that either. I meant what I said, you know that." Kamren chuckled, reaching for the pillow and neatly folded blanket on the edge on the bed. She walked over Brody and shoved it into his hands. Then she pointed to the door to signal him to leave out.

"Well, what's the case, Brody? You are a fucking stick up guy and you enjoy that shit!"

"I don't enjoy it, don't say that." Brody dropped the pillow and blanket, then sat on the bed. He dropped his head and began to rub the back of his neck. All the commotion from the stick up gave him a headache. Kamren's yelling wasn't making his headache any better.

"If you don't enjoy it, stop doing it. It's that simple, but you make it harder than what it is. I have one question and you better give me the right answer."

"What is it?" Brody asked.

"Why do you do it, Brody? I see so much potential in you, it hurts to see you live like this. Your mom, she worries about you so much. I'm tired of lying to her about everything. Don't get me started on your dad! He can sense my lies from a mile away, but he doesn't say much."

"Kamren, you ask me this question all the time and I tell you the same answer. I thought you were going to ask me something different this time."

"Oh yea, I forgot. You do it for the 'money.'" She smirked.

"What's with the air quotations, Kamren? Huh?"

"You and I BOTH know why you really do it!! You enjoy killing people. You love to hear another human being scream and beg for their fucking life. You sick and twisted bastard. If it wasn't for love, I wouldn't let you nowhere around me."

"What, you can't be serious right now? What kind of person do you really think I am?"

"You're the grim reaper, that's who you are!!! People just drop dead when you're around." Brody walked towards Kamren with his arms open, she stared him up and down.

"Brody, please don't take another step closer to mee." Kamren wiggled her shoulders and brushed Brody away. He was a little insulted, but he did exactly what she said. He knew Kamren was upset and he didn't want to add more fuel to the fire.

"Baby, can you please calm down? I'm trying to have a normal conversation with you."

"No, Brody, I can't calm down. There is nothing normal about this conversation. I was worried sick about you, but that doesn't bother you. I called your phone so many times, but you didn't answer. I thought…" Kamren shook her head and sat on the bed. Within seconds, the tears began to stream down her oval shaped face. The thought of Brody being lying somewhere in a pull of blood, ripped her heart in pieces.

"You thought what? Talk to me." Brody slowly walked towards Kamren. Once he was close enough to her he wrapped his arms around her. Kamren fell on her back and cried harder.

"I thought you were dead, Brody. Why would you not answer the phone?" Kamren covered her face, so Brody couldn't see the snot running out of her nose.

"I'm sorry, I didn't think news would travel that fast. I really thought you were at work and you wouldn't hear anything."

"Well you were wrong. I thought I was going to see you rolling in on a stretcher. I love you, Brody and you're my world. I only want the best for you. I'm starting to think you don't want the best for yourself. You know my dad can easily get you on at his job."

"I'm sorry, baby, but laying bricks and pouring cement isn't my cup of tea." Brody rubbed the back of his head again. When he knew he was wrong, it was the first thing he did. Kamren sucked her teeth and push him off her.

"Oh, but killing people is your cup of tea? Seriously, Brody, get out of this room. You're like two seconds from getting put out of this house!"

"Can you please stop screaming like a crazy woman? You know what I want to do with my life. I just need time to get out of the game first. It takes time to get your shit together. Not everyone is born with a silver spoon in their mouth like you. I have to grind and get mines out the mud."

"Shut up, Brody, just shut the fuck up! We've been together for six years and I've been hearing that same shit for the past two years. That's twenty-four months of giving me the run around. You don't want to get out of the game, because you, ACTUALLY, don't want to get out the game!! As long as you have Savage, True Love, and Big Head, you'll do this shit forever."

"You act like it's easy to wake up one day and say I'm out of the game. It's like once you're a jack boy, you're always a jack boy."

"Brody, you're supposed to MAKE it easy. I'm going to my parent's house tonight and that's not up for debate. I'll call you tomorrow, the next day, or whatever."

"Aaww, come on, baby, don't go to your parents. You know what they're going to think." Brody said.

"WHY NOT, BRODY, HUH?"

"Can you please stop shouting and talk normal?"

"I ask you to do a lot of things, but you don't do it. Why should I listen to you, what makes you so special?"

"Because I'm your man and you love me." Brody said.

"Miss me with that love shit. If you love me, you wouldn't do have of the shit you do. What if someone tries to harm me because of something YOU did? Every night I pray for our safety because of the things YOU do in the streets!!"

"Well, clearly, your prayers are working. Nothing has happened, or nothing will happen, chill out, bruh. You're giving me a damn headache, Kamren." Brody's loud outburst startled Kamren, but she wasn't going to shut up. She had a lot to get off her chest and he had no other option, but to listen.

"Fuck you, Brody, you're so damn dumb!"

"You know what? I'm straight on this conversation." Jumping to his feet, but slowly pacing through the room. Brody didn't want to say too much, but Kamren pushed every button, pissing him off.

"What happened?" Kamren asked.

"What do you mean what happened? What happened with what, Kamren?" Brody asked.

"What happened tonight?"

"Do you remember when I told you Savage got jacked?" He asked.

"Yea, didn't they take like $2,000 and a bunch of guns?" Kamren asked.

"Yea, well, that's what we handled. After that, we drove to Baton Rouge and we turned around. That's it, baby, now, can we end this conversation?"

"You'll never become the mayor of Opelousas if you continue to live like this. For some odd reason, you have a clean record. Before you know it, you're going to fuck it up. Tomorrow is the big cook-out, I'll tell my mom I'm staying over to help her. What time are you coming over? You know my dad is going to want to watch the game with you."

"Damn, about that, I won't be able to make it. You know how it is after we do a stick up."

"Yea, I know exactly how it is. You leave town for a few days and come home like everything is cool. I'll see you whenever I see you." Kamren grabbed her duffle bag and gave Brody the peace sign. She didn't want a hug, a kiss, or any type of affection from him. The only thing Brody could do is follow behind Kamren and close the door.

Once she pulled off, he punched the wall and his fist went through it. Brody was angry with himself for the fact that he left Kamren leave like that. He couldn't say anything, Brody could tell Kamren was slowly reaching her breaking point. He had to do something, soon, or he would lose the only woman he ever loved.

Even though Brody wasn't living a good life, he had goals and tons of ambition. Since he was six years old, he wanted to follow in his grandfather's footsteps. Brody Samuel Cotton Senior, was the major of Opelousas, years ago. He won two elections in a row. Brody always looked up to his grandfather and not his father. His father was content with the comfortable lifestyle of collecting a check from social security.

Brody use to spend hours with Brody Senior campaigning, in his office, and making appearances. He loved the power he saw his grandfather had and the way he impacted the community. Brody wanted the same thing, until he found himself tied into the streets. He always told his friends about his dream, but they laughed. The only person that took him seriously was Savage. That's because Savage had big dreams of his own of being a photographer. He wanted to travel and let the world see his talent through his lens. Despite how True Love and Big Head didn't believe in them, they still held onto their dreams.

Brody sat on the couch and buried his face into the palm of his hands. He always got a thrill when killing someone, but Kamren always killed his high.

"Why the fuck do I always do this?" Brody slapped his head four times, sighing. Reaching for his phone to call Savage, but he was calling Brody. He answered the call and said, "talk to me."

"I need to come over, Rachel put me out."

"I was just about to call you. Kam and I got into a huge argument and she left. She's going to her parents' house and that will only make it worse!"

"Damn, I guess tonight isn't our night, I'm coming over." Savage said. He stood outside of his car, smoking his last cigarette. He had to calm down before he would explode on his girlfriend. Even though he was in the wrong, he felt she had no solid reason to put him out of the house. It was actually his house, but he didn't argue with her. He grabbed a few pieces of clothing as ran out of the house. He wanted to get out her face, fast.

"Bet."

***

After calling her best friend, and crying for an hour, Kamren finally made it to her parent's house. She stood at the door with her bag and she could smell the delicious aroma of lemon pies.

Janice opened the door and said, "hey, baby, what are you doing here?"

"Hey, Ma, I came to help you cook." She laughed. She prayed her mom didn't see the lies through her red eyes.

"Aaww, thank you, baby, but you didn't have to. I know you worked the late shift," Janice grabbed Kamren's duffle bag and pulled her into the house.

"I'm not worrying about that, Mom. I would love to help you guys. Besides, I'm starving, I didn't have time to cook. I know you have some type of leftovers." Kamren laughed.

"I sure do, there's chicken pasta in the icebox."

"Oh good, my favorite." Janice and Kamren walked into the kitchen and she went straight to the icebox. She rubbed her hands together and pulled the pot of pasta out. She could feel her mom staring at her, so she turned around.

"What, Mom?" She asked.

"Where is Brody?"

"Oh, he's at home." Kamren said.

"Oh okay, why isn't he with you?" Janice asked.

"Because I want to help you, I told you that, Mom." Kamren turned around and grabbed a spoon. She scooped a large amount to pasta into the glass bowl, then she placed it into the microwave.

One thing about the streets in Opelousas, they talked a lot. Sometimes, they talked too much, plus, no one minded their own business. It was no secret what Brody did for a living, but no one in Kamren's family spoke about it. She was glad they never did, it was an awkward situation to talk about.

"Okay, Kamren, I just asked a question. Is he coming tomorrow?" Janice asked.

"Uhh, I don't think so. He has to take his sister to that thing." Thirty seconds later, the microwave beeped, and she pulled her bowl out. Her mom watched every move she made. Kamren shook her head and blew the steam that was coming from her bowl.

"What thing?"

"A party or something, Mom, I don't remember what he said. Brody tells me a lot of things and I can't remember every detail."

"Okay, Kamren, but did you hear about that shooting? There was a girl involved in it and it made the news already."

"What do you mean, a girl?" Kamren asked.

"Well, actually two girls were involved. They were shot right along with four men. There aren't any leads yet, but I hope they catch the killers." Kamren had a feeling her mom didn't mean that and was just trying to make conversation. Janice could bet any amount of money that Brody was the shooter, or one of the shooters.

"Hhmm, poor them, things are getting crazy in Opelousas. Every time you look, it's a murder, or crime, going on." Kamren swallowed a spoon full of the pasta and reached the icebox for a bottle of water.

"I know, sometimes, I'm scared to leave the house."

"Same here, Mom, same here."

Five minutes later, her father, Gary, walked into the kitchen. He was a little surprised to see Kamren out at this time, and especially without Brody.

"Hey, baby girl, what are you doing here?" Gary gave Kamren a smile and reached for a chocolate chip cookie. Janice gave him the side eye and he quickly dropped the cookie. Kamren laughed, but she didn't understand why her father dropped the cookie.

"Gary, don't try it."

"Aww, Janice, it's just one cookie." Gary pouted.

"You can have cookies today, or tomorrow, but not both. You don't get any days both with this diet." Janice said.

"Dad, you're on a diet, since when?" Kamren asked.

"Since Monday, your mom put me on a diet," Gary stared at the cookies and licked his lips. He could taste the chocolates dancing on his tongue. He hadn't had a sweet all week, and he was about to go crazy.

"I could see why, look at that stomach, Dad. Did it grow over night, or something?" Kamren rubbed her dad's big stomach, laughing. He did the same thing and laughed as well.

"I think so, because I don't remember this happening."

"I remember when it happened, but I'm going to fix it. I refuse to let my husband die from obesity." Janice reached in the fridge and grabbed a small container of carrots. She handed the container to Gary and he rolled his eyes.

"Where is Brody, baby?" Gary asked.

"Home." She said.

"Oh, okay, I'm surprised you two aren't together."

"We're not twins, Dad, we don't spend every moment together." She chuckled.

"I know, baby, but that is your boyfriend. I can't wait until he becomes your husband." Gary smiled.

"I hope that day comes soon. I would love to see you in a beautiful white gown." Janice smiled.

"How long have you two been together?" Gary asked. Kamren dropped her bowl on the counter and exhaled.

"We've been together eight years, Dad, eight, long, years."

"In that time, you could have gotten married twice." Gary laughed.

"I know, Dad, but I can't rush anything with him, or anyone else, for that matter."

"What's the problem, Kamren, he isn't ready?" Gary asked.

"I'm not sure, Dad, you have to ask him that. I can't speak for anyone, but myself."

No one knew it, but Brody proposed to Kamren twice. Both times, she told him yea, but never went through with it. Brody was ready to marry her, but he wasn't ready to change his life completely around. Kamren wanted it all and not just a ring. If a marriage couldn't change Brody, she wasn't sure what would change him.

Talking about marriage wasn't something Kamren liked. It always made her feel uncomfortable and out of place. Right now, Brody was good, but he wasn't good enough to marry.

"I sure will ask him tomorrow. It's time for him to pop the big question or keep it pushing. We don't need any kids out of wedlock over here."

"You won't see him tomorrow and if he isn't ready, ole well. Not everyone was raised like how you guys raised me." Kamren was raised in the church and to do the right things. Majority of her relatives were married, had kids, or married. Their spouses had jobs and weren't in the streets like Brody. Sometimes, Kamren felt left out, because she couldn't relate to them.

Brody also wanted a child, but Kamren wasn't ready for that either. She was scared that something would happen to Brody and she would have to raise her child alone.

"Why isn't he coming? He always come to the family cook-out. He's basically a part of the family." He chuckled.

"He's taking his little sister somewhere tomorrow."

"Oh, okay, but honestly, when will you two get married and have a baby?"

"I don't know, Dad, whenever Brody gets it together."

"Gets what together, Kamren?" Gary asked. Kamren was slowly getting annoyed with her father's question. They often had this conversation and she hated.

"His life, Dad, and I'm not rushing him into anything."

"So, you're just going to date him forever?" Janice asked.

"Oh my God, no disrespect, but I don't want to talk about him right now."

"Every time we have this conversation you say that. What exactly are you two doing, besides shacking up?"

"Gary, that's enough!" Janice shouted. Kamren wasn't bothered by her father's words. She chuckled and took one more bite of the pasta. She used her hand to wipe her mouth and placed the bowl in the sink. Janice tried to stop Kamren from walking away, but Kamren shook her head.

"You want to know something, Dad, not ever one is like you. Despite what you heard about Brody, or how you feel about him, he's a good guy. He isn't perfect, but I love him. Like you told me before, you can't help who you fall in love with. When it comes to Brody and me, you don't believe that. That makes you a hypocrite, and you know it."

"Kamren, watch your mouth!" Janice shouted.
"You know what, Mom, I'm just going to go back home."

"No, baby, don't go."

"Let her leave, Janice, let her! When it comes to that Brody boy, she doesn't like hearing the truth." Gary said.

"No, Dad, I know the truth, but it's YOU, who can't handle the truth. Goodnight, Mom, I'll call you when I make it home." Kamren kissed her mom on the cheek and walked out of the kitchen. Gary didn't bother to stop her and that made Janice pissed.

Kamren grabbed her duffle bag and rushed out of the house. She didn't want her mom to follow her out of the house and make a big scene. Kamren respected her father, but she felt like he thought he was perfect. He had all the answers, but she didn't want them all. Whatever decision she made with Brody, was between her and Brody. Not her, her father, and Brody.

Kamren got into her car and sped off. She thought about calling Brody, but she changed her mind. He was partially the reason for the argument. She reached for her phone and called Valerie.

Valerie seemed like she was up and moving around. She cleared her throat a little and said, "talk to me, Kamren."

"What are you doing, Val?" Kamren asked.

"Running on my treadmill, but what's up?" Valerie turned the treadmill off and reached for the cold bottle of water. She didn't hesitate to pop the top off, drowning her mouth with water. Water entered her nose, but she didn't care. She reached for her towel and wiped her face.

"Girl, I need to come over. My dad and I got into an argument."

"What, for what?" Valerie asked.

"What else?"

"Brody?" She asked.

"Of course, the usual argument. I'm so tired of this, Val, it's the same fucking argument! My family ask the same questions over, and over. Everyone makes comments about Brody. I'm the one defending him, but he's never around to defend himself. This is bullshit, Val, and I'm tired of it."

"I know, girl, but you need to calm down. I don't want you to wreck or anything."

"You're right, but I would like to drive this car into my house." Kamren laughed.

"Girl, don't do that, that's a nice house." Valerie laughed.

"It is, huh? But I'm so angry right now, UUGGHHHHH!!!"

"Where is Brody anyways?" Valerie asked.

"I don't know, they probably left already."

"Did he say where they were going?" Valerie asked.

"No, and I didn't bother asking him. Open the door, I'm outside," Kamren turned left on Jake Drive, and pulled into the first driveway.

"Okay." Kamren grabbed her purse and turned her car off. She was happy to see that Valerie's boyfriend wasn't home. It was pitch dark outside so rushed out of her car. Valorie Simone was a twenty-four-year-old up and coming make-up artist. She was like Valorie's personal stylist and Kamren loved it. Valerie and Kamren were also best friends. She used to date Savage, but that ended after two months. Unlike Kamren, she couldn't handle a street nigga and ended things with him.

"Hey, boo." Valerie said.

"Hey, girl, what's up." Kamren said.

Valerie stood in the doorframe, sweaty, and with bottle of water in her hand. Valerie was a fitness queen and had the body of a goddess. Her arms were extended open waiting to give Kamren.

Kamren gave Valorie a hug and walked into the house. She dropped her duffle bag on the floor and sat on the couch. Valerie sat next to Kamren and asked, "are you okay?"

"No, not really, but I'll be okay. It's starting to get overwhelming, Val, and I'm getting to my breaking point with Brody."

"I know, baby, but you can't break down like this. You need to talk to Brody and tell him how you feel." Valerie said.

"I have talked to him about it, but it feels like I'm talking to a brick wall. He says he loves me, but he doesn't want to change."

"I know Brody well, he wants to change. He has to change on his own time. You can stand by his side, or you can leave him. Either way, he's going to change when HE'S ready."

"That's the thing, Val, I don't see it happening anytime soon. I love him, but I don't know what to do anymore. It's slap in the face when my family ask me when Brody and I are getting married."

"Let's be honest, Kam, you're the reason you two aren't married."

"No, he's the reason we're not married, not me. I won't, and I refuse to marry someone who's heavy in the streets. I don't want to marry him one day, then, the next, he's gone." She said.

"Gone like how?"

"Prison or jail, I can't do it, my heart won't allow me to do. I need Brody to fully turn his life around before we take a step like that. That's a huge step, Valerie, and I will not play with God like that. I will not get in front of my family and friends like that and pretend I'm ready for that."
"Maybe getting married will change him." Valerie said.

"No, it doesn't work like that. At the end of the day, I can't marry him under these circumstances."

"Okay, but like I told you before, you have two options. You can leave, or you can stay, but let's be honest. Brody is a damn good man and he loves you dearly. That boy would literally, take a bullet for you. If you leave him, the next women will slide in your place. Nine out of ten, she's going to accept his lifestyle until he changes. Before you decide, Kam, think long and hard about it. These bitches want what you have, you know that."

"Maybe you're right," Kamren rubbed her bare face and turned away.

"If you don't want to go home, you know you can crash on the couch."

"Thanks girl, where's Tyson?" Kamren asked.

"He's at work, but he gets off at 6:00 am."

"Oh, okay."

"Well, let me get back to my workout. There is grilled chicken and carrots on the stove," Valerie patted her on the back and stood to her feet. She stepped on her treadmill and pressed the on button. Kamren hated to admit it, but majority of what Valerie said was right. On the other hand, she couldn't understand how Valerie could say some of the things she said. A man should change before marriage, and not after.

Chapter 2

"What are you doing?" Brody pinned his phone against his ear with his shoulder as he talked. Kamren stared in the bathroom mirror, adjusting her hair, while flossing her teeth. For thirty minutes, her and Brody were on the phone, but it wasn't much conversation between the two of them. For majority of the time, she ignored him, and gave him one-word answers. Brody could sense the animosity in her voice. He was trying to find every way to make her happy, but nothing was working.

"Fixing my hair in the mirror." Kamren snapped. Brody silently exhaled and shook his head.

"Oh okay, who are you trying to get all cute for? I'm not there." He laughed, but Kamren didn't. His laughter slowly faded away.

"That's the point, because you're NOT here. You never know who comes to the barbeque today." Kamren laughed, in a high pitch. She was trying her best to piss him off, and he was.

"Kamren, I know you're upset with me, but don't try yourself."

"Brody Cotton Junior, is that a threat?" She smirked.

"Kamren, take it how you want. You know how I get down, I don't do threats, baby."

"You should know I'm not them niggas in the streets who fear you. You better watch your choice of words, Brody. I think you almost lost your damn mind." Kamren said.

"Yea, and I think you lost your mind, right along with me." Brody said.

"Whatever." She rolled her neck.

"What time are you going back home?" He asked.

"I don't know, I might stay out all night." She laughed.

"What?" Brody asked.

"I want to be like you."

"What the fuck that's supposed to mean, Kamren?" Brody asked, but it made Kamren laugh even more.

"It means, I want to stay out all night. I can do whatever I want and whenever I want."

"Whatever, Kamren, you're tripping on me because I didn't come to a damn cook-out!!"

"IT'S NOT ABOUT THE COOK-OUT, BRODY. YOU AND I KNOW IT'S WAAAYYYYY PASS THAT, SO DON'T PLAY DUMB! I have to go, have fun wherever you are." Kamren rubbed a little lip gloss on her lips while disconnecting the call. Brody called back, but she ignored the call. Kamren walked out of the bathroom and entered the living room. The house was packed with several of her family members. Some sat at the table playing booray and talking loud. Others sat in the dining room watching the football game. It was the Denver Broncos versus the Jacksonville Jaguars and everyone was cheering for the Broncos. The Broncos were winning by a field goal. By the way the Jaguars were playing, everyone knew the Broncos were going to win the game.

Majority of the women were outside gossiping and laughter among one another. Kamren hugged a few of her aunties and gave the small conversation.

"Kamren, girl, you're looking good," her Aunt Monica, slapped her on her ass, and laughed. Kamren was bashful, but she did a little spin for her aunties.

"Who me? I've been doing a little working out. My friend Valorie, is a workout freak!" She laughed.

"Well, I need to work out with your friend. Your waist is so tiny and perfect."

"I remember when I was small like that. Baby, those were the days, I tell you. All the boys at Carter High School wanted me," Kamren's aunt, Racheal, held her wide hips and flipped her hair. Kamren and Monica laughed.

"That was a long time ago." Monica laughed.

"I'll talk to you guys later, I need to holla at Jackie," Kamren grabbed her plate of food and kissed both her aunties.

It was a cool, sunny, day, even though it was the middle of January. Louisiana's weather was bipolar, you never know what to expect. Everyone sat outside enjoying the fresh air and delicious barbeque Kamren's parent's prepared. Her and her father said a few words to each, but they didn't make big conversation. Her mom didn't like the tension between the two, but she couldn't say much. Gary and Kamren were grown adults and had to make peace on their own.

"Where's Brody?" Jackie asked Kamren. Kamren continued to eat her potato salad and ignored Jackie. A few seconds later, Jackie tapped Kamren on the shoulder.

"Kamren, where's Brody?"

"Oh, I'm sorry, Jack, I was daydreaming. What did you ask me?" Kamren asked.

"I ask you where is Brody? I haven't seen him yet or heard his loud mouth." She laughed.

"That's because he isn't here, something came up with his sister."

"Oh, okay, well tell him I said hey. We're going back to Blanch tomorrow afternoon. Hopefully, I see him before we leave." Jackie was Kamren's cousin on dad's side of the family. She had a boyfriend and a six month of baby girl, but that didn't mean anything. Her and her boyfriend openly cheated on one another. Jackie didn't want to be with him, but she only stuck around because of the baby.

"He should be back by then." Kamren said.

"Is he still best friends with that True Love?" Jackie bit her bottom lip and smiled. Kamren dropped her fork and gave her a stale face. Within seconds, they both laughed.

"Yes, and leave True Love's crazy ass where he's at."

"Hell no, his ass is too fine to stay away. I follow him on Facebook and I stalk all his pictures." She laughed.

"I low-key don't like him." Kamren said.

"Why not?" Jackie asked.

"Because he's bad news and he calls Brody, 'B-more careful.' I hate that stupid hood shit, and Brody knows it."

"What, why does he call him that?" She asked and laughed.

"Because, one-time, Brody almost shot him with a gun three years ago. Since then, that's been his nickname. I think True Love knows I hate it, and he only calls Brody that when I'm around."

"I want to call True Love zzadddddyyyyy, tell him I said what's up." She laughed.

"I guess I'll tell him when I see him."

Besides Valerie, Jackie was the closest thing to Kamren. She often told her things about what Brody did in the streets. Jackie was easy to talk and didn't judge him by what he done.

"Are you okay, Kam, you seem a little off?"

"Yea, I'm good."

"Are you sure, you know you can talk to me?"

"Come by the house and we'll talk later. I don't want to talk over here," Kamren rolled her eyes and pointed at her dad. He was standing in front of the grill while flipping the hamburger patties. He seemed so happy and unbothered with everything.

"Oh Lord, what did he say, or do?"

"Same ole shit with Brody and I'm tired of it!" Kamren spoke, in a loud whisper. Just because her dad was five feet away at the grill, she didn't want to talk loud.

"Brody is a thug and your dad needs to accept. You two have been together for like eight years. He's going to change when he's ready. Not when anyone else want him to. That goes for you too, Kamren, you can't force him."

"What? I'm not forcing him. I'm only trying to guide him to the right path! The path that he wants to go down. Since his father is a piece of shit man, Brody is the next person in line to take on the tradition to become mayor. One fuck-up can mess all that up and he knows that. He's aware of that, but he still hasn't gotten his shit together. I really don't know what to do anymore, Jackie, I'm running out of options."

"Well, seems like you have one more problem." Jackie said.

"What's that?" Jackie pointed to Brody, who was standing at the back door. He had a white Styrofoam cup in one hand and a bouquet in the other. The arrangement of hot pink roses, orange Asiatic lilies, medium sunflowers, and lavender stock, were beautiful. Brody's white and orange shirt went well with the arrangement.

Kamren wanted to smile, but she didn't. On the other hand, she was surprised that Brody was here. Jackie waved at him and he nodded his head. He glanced at Kamren and smiled.

"Aaawww, he brought you flowers."
"So what?" Kamren asked.

"Come on, Kam, don't act like that with him. I thought he was out of town?" Jackie asked.

"I thought so too, girl."

"Well, clearly, he didn't go, so that means he's trying."

"I guess." Brody grabbed Kamren's arm and said, "hey, baby."

"What up, B, or should I say, Mr. B-More careful?" Kamen sized Brody up and down and stood to her feet. Brody and Jackie smacked their lips, but Kamren didn't care.

"Stop being mean, Kamren, hey, Brody."

"Thanks, Jack, what's up?" Brody asked.

"Nothing much, Kamren and I were just talking about True Love. How has he been?" Jackie twirled her leg and smiled. Kamren flared her nose and chuckled.

"He's aiight, but I'll tell him you asked about him."

"It'll be nice if you told him today, like, right now." She laughed.

"Okay, I'll do that." Brody laughed, and placed the cup on the bench. He handed Kamren the flowers and kissed her forehead. She inhaled the fresh scent of the flowers and placed them on the bench.

"Thank you, they're nice." She said.

"You're welcome, baby, anything for you." He smiled. Brody dug into his pocket and pulled his phone out. He sent True Love a text message, then he turned the phone screen to Jackie. She tossed her hands in the air and laughed.

"Thanks, B, I owe you."

"It's all good, you don't owe me anything. Kamren, can we talk for a minute?" Brody asked.

"I guess, Brody. I'll be right back, Jackie."

"Okay." Jackie said.

Brody and Kamren walked away from the crowd and entered the laundry room. It was clean, spacious, and smelled like lavender Purex. Kamren leaned against the dryer, standing face, to face, with Brody. She wasn't going to say anything until he started talking.

"How are you?" Brody asked.

"I'm fine, Brody, but what about you?"

"I'm good, I'm good, I missed you last night. When I got back home, you weren't there."

"I told you I was going to my parents, but that changed. I stay at Val's house last night." Kamren said.

"Why?" Brody asked.

"Because my dad and I got into an argument. I'm tired of defending you, Brody, I really am. My dad is always asking me the same question and I give him the same answers. Those same answers lead to the same damn argument. It doesn't matter how many times I try and dodge it. It leads the same shit. Majority of the time, I'm defending you alone." Kamren pushed Brody into the wall, then she pushed him again. His back was against the wall, he couldn't do anything. Even if his back wasn't against the wall, he still wouldn't have done anything.

"Kamren, what questions did he ask you? The same bullshit about us not being married?"

"Yes!"

"That's on you, you're the one who basically turned me done. You turned me down not once, but twice. I wish you would tell everyone that, but you don't."

"Telling them that doesn't change anything." Kamren shouted.

"Yes, it does, it could change how they feel about me. That's majority of the reason they don't like me."
"No, it's because you're in the street, don't play crazy, Brody!"

"Look, fuck the reason they don't like me. You like me, and that's all that matters."

"It does matter." Kamren said.

"Why does it matter, Kamren? Don't I make you happy? Don't I love you unconditionally? Most of these niggas have their girlfriends out here looking a fool, but not me. Why can't you accept the fact that I do what I do. When the change comes, it's going to come. We've been together for how long, and you wait 'til now to start pressuring me? That is crazy, and it came out of the left field."

"Whoa, whoa, whoa, wait a minute, Brody Cotton! Just because you don't cheat on me, doesn't give you the right to have me worrying sick about you. When I'm at work, and I hear a black male was shot, my heart drops to the floor. I never know if it's going to be you on the stretcher. So, excuse the hell out of me for caring that much about you. For the last THREE years, we've been going through this. Now I'm reaching my breaking point. Every time you read the newspaper or watch the news it's the same thing. Another black male was shot or killed. Another black male killed or shot someone!!!! I DON'T WANT THAT TO BE YOU, BRODY, I DON'T WANT THAT TO BE YOU!" Kamren shouted, but her soft voice started to crack.

She buried her face into her hands and sobbed. Hearing Kamren cry always made Brody sad. Even if he wasn't the person causing the tears. He slowly walked to her and held her tight.

"You just don't understand, Brody. I love you so much. You're the only guy who's ever treated me like this. If something happens to you, I won't know what I would do. You'll never understand how I feel when I approach the stretchers at work. Last week, a guy died while being transported to the hospital. He had the same shoes on as you. I dropped to the floor and my body went numb."

"What, why didn't you tell me this, baby?" He asked.

"Because I knew you would say I was overreacting."

"Kamren, you have to stop thinking the worse. Nothing will happen to me, I know how to stick and move. Besides, I have my eyes on the big picture." He laughed.

Kamren wrapped her arms around Brody's neck and she started to kiss him. It didn't matter how much she wanted to stay upset with Brody, she couldn't. She loved Brody with all her heart, and all she wanted was the best for him.

"I believe in you, baby, and I can't wait to see you fulfill your dream."

"After that, I may run for senator, vice president, or even president." He laughed.

"Whew, that's a big step, but I think I can do it. I have you by my side, I can do anything I put my mind to." He smiled.

"I like the way that sounds, it's picture perfect. Really, Brody, why are you so heavy in the streets? Why are you so comfortable living this way?"

"When I was growing up, my father was a bum ass nigga. He didn't care about much. As long as the minimum bills were paid, he was good. I couldn't get a job when I was younger, so I picked up a pistol. For me, jacking was easier than selling drugs. I didn't have to stand on the block and slang rocks. In my eyes, I felt like I would be dangling my freedom over my head. When I did my first jacking, it was bittersweet. Having that power of making someone throw their hands in the air felt good. I remember that shit like it was yesterday, I was only thirteen. The bitter part was when I was running. Feeling that cold pistol against my skin didn't feel good. I can't lie, I hated it, but after a while, it became normal. My pistol was a part of me and I carried it everywhere I went. I want to give you the world, baby, but this shit is addictive. I just pray that you don't leave me before I get my shit together."

"I don't know, Brody, I talk a lot of shit. At the end of the day, I can't let you go."

***

Brody sat on the park bench staring into space. The weather was cool, but it good enough to enjoy a day outside. Kamren was at work, so he decided to take his little sister to the park. In Brody's eyes, Natasha is the sunshine on a rainy day. She was only six years old, but their bond was amazing. She also shared special bond with Kamren, as well. Brody was her only sibling, so she considered Kamren as her big sister. Brody loved the relationship Natasha and Kamren shared.

"Brody, come and play with me." Natasha waved at Brody as her and another kid went up and down on the see-saw. Brody smiled and slid his phone into his pocket. He was texting Big Head, but that wasn't important right now. He stood to his feed and jogged to his sister. The closer Brody got to Natasha, the bigger her smile grew.

"Hey, baby girl." Brody said.

"Brody, can we go on the swing?" Natasha asked.

"Of course, we can." The other little girl slowly climbed off the see-saw. Brody opened his arms and Natasha jumped into them. They both laughed and walked to the swings. Natasha jumped out of his arms and sat on the swing. She pointed to the swing next to her and Brody sat down. Natasha swung at her fast pace, but Brody swung at a slow pace. A lot was on his mind and he was slightly distracted.

The conversation he had with Kamren was two days ago, but it was still on his mind.

"Brody, can we get pizza after this?"

"We sure can." He said.

"Can we bring Kam Kam some at work? She loovveeessss cheese pizza."

"Yea, we can, but do you want to do to Pizza-Hut?" Brody asked.

"Yes, they have the best pizza!" She shouted and laughed.

"I'm glad to know pizza make you excited and not boys." Brody laughed.

"I'm not worrying about boys, Brody. You're the only boy I love. When I get older, I'm going to marry a man just like you." She laughed.

"Just like me?" He chuckled.

"Yep." Natasha said.

"Why like me, what makes me so special?" Brody asked.

"Because you're smart, you're funny, you love me, and you always buy me nice things. I wish Daddy was like you." Natasha slowly stopped swinging and a frown took over her face. It was no secret that Brody Junior wasn't happy about having another child so late in his marriage. He sort of, disliked Natasha, and every one saw it. That was the prime reason he didn't like his father, Natasha was innocent in a situation she had no control of.

"Don't worry about that, baby, I love you, and that's all that matters."

"I know, and I love you more. I wish Papa was still here, he loved coming to the park." Natasha said.

"He did, but always know this, he's here with us all the time. Even when you think he isn't around, he is."

"How do you know that?" She asked.

"Because he's our guardian angel and it's his job to always be around." Brody said.

"Brody, what's a guardian angel?"

"A guardian angel is someone who's in Heaven and they watch over you. They shield you from all the bad that tries to come your way. When I die, I'm going to be your guardian angel. I promise I won't let anything or anyone harm you."

"I don't want you to die, I'm going to be sad." She said.

"I know, but we all have to die one day. Let's not talk about that, because I don't want to make you sad."

"Okay, but I'm going to miss you when you die."

"I know, baby, and I'm going to miss you too." Brody leaned to the side and kissed his sister's rosy cheek. She blushed and covered her gapped tooth. Every time she hid her gapped tooth, Brody removed her hand. He always told her to embrace her gap tooth and never be embarrassed of it.

"Brody, can we fix my teeth?" Natasha asked.

"If you want to, but you have to wait two more years."

"Aw, man, okay, until then, I'll eat all the popcorn I can. I can't wait to see that new movie Sunday." Brody's eyes grew big once he was reminded of their Sunday plans. Since Natasha was four years old, her and Brody attended the movies every Sunday. It was something they both enjoyed doing, especially Natasha. It was just another way for her to spend time with Brody despite his busy schedule.

"Damn, about that, I'm going to have to cancel are date, baby girl."

"What, why? You've never cancelled on me before." Natasha jumped off the swing and stood in front of Brody. By the way her arms were folded across her chest, he knew she was upset with him. He tried to grab her hand, but she took a step back.

"I know, and I'm sorry, Natasha. Something important came up and I have to handle it. We can go the next day, I promise. I'll pick you up from school and we can spend the whole day together. You can spend the night with Kamren and I. We can even get breakfast before I drop you to school. Wouldn't you like that, Natasha?" Brody asked.

"Yea, I would, but you've never cancelled our movie date. Is that thing more important than the movies?" Natasha asked.

"Of course not, but it's important. I need to handle this, it's like a job. Isn't your little friend having a pool party Sunday? I know you wouldn't to miss all that fun just to sit in the dark movies with me." Brody laughed. He hoped his words would make Natasha laugh, but it didn't. Her face dropped lower, and she shrugged her shoulders.

"Yea, but I like spending time with you, B." She said.

"I know, Natasha, but I promise, Monday we can do whatever you want."

"Whatever I want?" She asked.

"Yep and I'll ask Kamren to drop you to the party. If I'm back in time I'll pick you up, is that cool?" Brody asked.

"Yea, that's cool." Natasha mumbled. Brody felt bad, but he had to handle his business. He agreed to take a ride to Mississippi with True Love to exchange some guns. Majority of Brody's guns were dirty, and they needed to be exchanged, as well.

"Do you still love me?" Brody smiled and laughed. He knew cancelling plans wouldn't stop his sister from loving him. He still wanted to hear her say she loved them.

Instead of saying the words, she nodded her head up and down. Brody grabbed Natasha by the hand and gave her a hug.

"Aaaawwwww, that is so cute." Natasha's smile grew big and Brody turned around. It was Kamren standing behind him. Food stains were on her scrubs and her jacket was drapped over her arm. Natasha ran to Kamren and wrapped her arms around her hips.

"Hey, Kamren!"

"Hey, Natasha, seems like someone is happy to see me." Kamren laughed.

"She isn't the only person happy to see you. What are you doing here, I thought you got off at eight?"

"I was supposed to, but Daisy wanted to stay until eight. I figured I would surprise you two."

"Kamren, Brody said since we aren't going to the movies, you're dropping me to the party Sunday. Is that true?"

"Yea, but ONLY if your mom is okay with it." Kamren was a little confused, but she wasn't going to say anything in front of Natasha.

"Okay, as soon as I get home, I will ask her. Brody, can I go and finishing playing?" She asked.

"Yea, but in twenty minutes, we're leaving. You have school tomorrow and I don't want to hear mom's mouth." Natasha nodded her head and ran off. Kamren grabbed the swing and sat next to Brody. She looked to the left and stared at the elementary school. Thoughts of her childhood fluttered her brain and she laughed.

"What's funny, Kamren?" Brody asked.

"Do you remember the good ole days at North Elementary?" Kamren asked.

"Good ole days, what good ole days? Since the day I met you, you've been mean to me." He laughed.

"That's because in the third grade, girls ruled, and boys drooled." Kamren laughed and shook her head.

"You were so mean, but you were so cute. I remember when I proposed to you on the 2nd day of school, but you turned me down. I should've known back then, you didn't want to be my wife."

"Haha, very funny, Brody. You can't propose to a girl with a Ring Pop that you already licked on."

"Hey, be nice, it was the thought that counts." Brody smiled.

"Yea, it was, and you got an A for effort. Honestly, Brody, who would have thought we would be together? We were two snotty nose kids, playing in the sandbox. Back then, that was puppy love and now, it's real love."

"If you ask me, it was real love back then. I've had my share of women, but you're the only woman I can say I honestly love. It's something about you that I'll never find in another woman."

"I love you more, baby, and I'm glad you have common sense. I've seen the women in your past and none of them are fucking with me." She laughed.

"Yea, you're right about that."

"So, what's with this party Natasha is talking about?" Kamren asked.

"One of her friends from school is having a little pool party. I think it's her birthday party, but I'm not sure. I have to make a run with True Love Sunday, so I convinced her to go to the party."

"Sunday, as in, movie day, Sunday?" Kamren asked, but she knew the answer to her question.

"Yea, but I'm trying to be back by time the party ends. That way, I can pick her up, and kiss her ass all Monday." Brody laughed.

"I guess, Brody, but when were you going to tell me about this run with True Love?" Kamren asked.

"I was going to tell you tonight, baby. He told me this yesterday, please don't argue with me on this one." Brody begged.

"It's no argument, Brody, but I'm leaving." Kamren cracked a smile and stood to her feet. She wiped the back of her pants and walked away. Brody ran behind her and grabbed her shoulder. She ignored him and continued to walk away.

"Natasha, I'll see you later, okay, baby?" Kamren asked.

"Okay."

"Kamren, wait, why are you leaving?" Brody asked.

"I'm going to let you enjoy your day with your sister and I'm about two seconds from slapping you. I'm really about two seconds about slapping the taste out of your mouth, but your sister is present. See you later, B- More careful."

- -

Chapter 3

"Have y'all heard anything about the shooting?" Brody asked Savage.

"No, I haven't, but what about you?" Savage asked.

"Me either, I guess it's another cold case."

"It better be, we didn't leave any evidence behind. That black Yukon is now a white Yukon with a Florida license plate." He laughed.

"Rrrriiiiggghhhhhhhttttttttt."

Brody and Savage sat in his living room in a daze. They both were high and talking shit. The small living room was full of smoke and smelled only of marijuana. Brody took the advantage of getting high as a kite while he was away from home. Kamren didn't allow drugs into her home. Brody could hardly bring a pack of cigars or cigarettes with him. The police were always harassing Brody, so

Kamren don't want Brody to have a single thing on him when the police stop him.

Savage slanted eyes were practically closed, but that didn't stop him from lighting another blunt. Suddenly, purple clouds filled the living room. He took a puff on the blunt, then he passed it to Brody. Brody took one hit and began to cough. His cough was rough, and it sound as if mucus was sitting on his chest.

"Damn, B, pass my shit back to me," Savage extended his hand out and laughed. Brody continued to cough, as he passed the blunt back to Savage. He wiped his watery eyes and grabbed the family size of Starburst candy. He shuffled through the bag and grabbed a few.

"You can have that shit, Savage, after today, I'm done smoking."

"What?"

"That's what I said, and I mean it, this time." Brody said.

"Let me guess, Kamren threaten you too?" Savage asked.

"Yea, but not about smoking. I just think it's time to stop smoking. It's time to get my life together and I'm not saying this because I'm high, I'm saying this because it's true. Kamren is getting restless with this lifestyle, but I can't blame her either. Shit is getting crazy around here and never know who's next to be on a t-shirt."

"I don't blame you, I've been thinking the same thing. Since the shooting on the Compress Road, Toni and I haven't been seeing eye to eye. For the past week, she's been spending majority of the days at her parent's house. Once she gets home, she goes straight to the shower and bed. If I didn't know any better, I would think she was cheating." He laughed and hit the blunt.

"We both know Toni isn't crazy enough to cheat." Brody laughed.

"I'll burn the whole city down if I EVER find out she's cheating. My nigga, I'll start from Jefferson projects and ricochet it down Railroad Avenue." He laughed.

"What's crazy is that I believe you would do that. Seriously though, we need to get it together before it's too late. Do we really want to do this shit until we're old and gray? I'm pretty sure my aim won't be the same."

"I'm pretty sure I won't be able to carry a chopper anymore." Savage laughed.

"Rrriigghhhhtttt, I like the way you think. I can see it in Toni's eye she's getting disgusted with me. I hate that shit man, I can't do anything about it unless I change. That night I came home after the shooting, she didn't say a word to me. Toni had a pillow and blanket waiting for me on the couch." Savage shook his head and tapped the blunt into the ashtray. He was done smoking for the time being. He grabbed the bag on candy from Brody and poured a few in his hand. Within seconds he unwrapped the candies and tossed them into his mouth.

"Damn, Kamren is on the same shit. She was waiting for me at the top of the staircase. We got into an argument and she left. She already had it on her mind to leave for the night. I don't want to lose her, but like I told her, the streets are addictive." Brody said.

"You are right about that, my brother. I can't leave the house without that iron. Not because I need it, it's become a part of me." Savage said.

"So, what are we going to do about all of this?"

"We're going to change, before this shit changes us. I actually like my girlfriend, and I want to keep her." Savage laughed.

"What's up with Big Head and True Love?" Brody asked.

"What do you mean?" Savage asked.

"They act like it's a problem to change. Seems like they don't want better for us or anyone else."

"That's become they don't know anything, but the hood. I hate to admit it, but they will be stuck here. What's crazy is that they are fine with that. I love my niggas, but I can't stay here with my niggas."

"I hope they don't be our downfall one day." Savage said.

"I be damn if I let another man be my downfall. I'll let a female do that and be proud." Brody laughed, and wiped his sweaty hands on his black jeans. It was a little warm in the house, so he pulled his hoodie off. He tossed it on the floor, then he stood to his feet. He walked over to the x-box and pressed the power button.

Brody grabbed both game controllers and tossed one to Savage.

"Bet $50 I can beat you while I'm loaded."

"Bet $50, I'm loaded, with a tab in my system too. Bet $60 and a box of gars." Savage laughed and reclined his sit all the back. Brody chuckled and increased the volume on the television. Every week he played Madden NFL 13 with Savage, and Savage lost. Savage didn't care though, ever week he thought he would beat Brody.
"Think fast!" Brody said. Savage eyes grew big and he dropped his blunt on the floor. He grabbed the controller and said, "quick hands, B, quick hands."

"You should have played football." Brody laughed.

"I am, right now, let me get the Broncos this rip."

"Naw, you already know that's my team."

"Damn, man, you know there are other teams?" Savage laughed. He scrolled through the football teams and chose the Steelers.

"You could have Romo, Peyton, Eli, and Brady, on one team, and you still wouldn't beat me."

"Don't speak too fast, I'm feeling lucky today. Put your money on the table." Savage reached into his deep pockets and pulled out a large amount of money. He rumbled through the money and dropped three twenty-dollar bills on the table. Brody pulled his wallet out and grabbed six ten-dollar bills. Savage glanced at his wallet and laughed.

"Man, besides my daddy and Papa, you're the only person I know that carry a wallet."

"So, what? Kamren brought this for me when she went to Tennessee."

"Aye, did Big Head tell you about that lick?" Savage asked.

"No, what lick?" Brody asked.

"His homie from New Roads need us to handle something for him."
"Oh yea, is money talking?" Brody asked.

"Three bodies and 4,000 for each head."

"Damn, that's not bad. This shit is easy money, I can't lie. You know Kamren asked me why I do this."

"What, are you for real?" Savage asked.

"Yea, that kind of messed my head up." Brody said.

"I bet it did, but what did you say?"

"I told her the truth, because selling drugs isn't for me." Savage and Brody locked eyes and laughed.

"Hell yea, that's the God's honest truth. Selling drugs, robbing, jacking, and being a shooter, isn't for everybody. At least you can admit that, some people can't. Look at Roy for example, he's been hustling since I was in elementary. What does he have to show for it? Not a got damn thing." Savage said.

"You're right about that, my brother. I don't have time to be on the block in the rain, sleet, and snow. Especially during the summer, I'm too light skin for that shit. I don't see how True Love does it. That nigga bleeds the block all day." He laughed.

"You won't ever see me riding around town with rocks on my lap. That's the stupidest thing I have ever heard of. I'll get a job before I sell dope, call me crazy. On a serious note, I've been searching schools for photography."

"Oh word, what did you find?" Brody asked.

"I see UL in Lafayette offers a degree in Visual Arts. I can concentrate in Photography and I may minor in New Media and Digital Art."

"That's what's up, Sav, you should do that, asap. We all know you have the brains to do whatever you want." Brody said.

"I just wish these other two fools would think like this. Big Head and True Love can't look further than a lick."

"I know, but one day, they'll get it together, hopefully."
"Can you really picture us being a photographer and a mayor? It sounds weird saying that."

"I can't lie, it does, but yea, I can. I remember when I was younger, I followed my grandfather everywhere. Sometimes, my mom would let me miss school just so I wouldn't miss his press conferences. I never understood how my dad never wanted to follow in his footsteps."
"That's because your dad is a square." Savage laughed.

"A bum ass square, I wish my mom would have never married him." Brody laughed.

"You sound a little bitter about that." Savage chuckled and remembered his blunt was on the floor. He paused the game and grabbed the blunt. Surprisingly, it was still burning, so he took a puff. He passed it to Brody, but he declined it.

"Naw, if she likes it, I love it."

Chapter 4

Kamren sat on the couch while rubbing her throbbing temples. She removed her leopard print glasses from her face and tossed them on the table. Today was a stressful day at work and days like this, made her reconsider her occupation. Two of her patients passed away today and it took a major toll on her. The patients were frequently in the hospital and Kamren sort of grew a bond with them.

Her phone started to ring and she quickly grabbed it. It was Brody's mom and she rolled her eyes. Majority of the time, Patty didn't have good things to say, but Kamren always answered her calls.

"Hey, Mrs. Patty, how are you?"

"I'm doing fine, but where is that son of mine? I hope he isn't out that acting like he has no home training." Patty's ignorant words made Kamren's skin crawl. She silently dropped her phone and tossed her hands in the air.

"Hello, Kamren, are you there?" Patty asked. Kamren grabbed her phone and exhaled.

"Brody is sleeping, Mrs. Patty, but when he wakes up, I'll tell him you called." Kamren lied without a problem. Brody wasn't home, but that was none of her business. If Kamren would have said he wasn't home, the conversation would have gone in a different direction. Kamren was not in the mood to hear how Brody needed to stay out of the streets and get his life together. Kamren was aware of all these things and didn't need to hear it from his mom every time she spoke to her.

"Okay, but, how are you? Did you work today?" Patty asked.

"Yes, ma'am, I got off about twenty minutes ago. It was a long and stressful day at work. Where is Natasha?" Kamren asked.

"She's playing in her room. I'll tell her you asked about her."

"Thank you, I'll talk to you later." Kamren said and disconnected the call.

The house was quiet and dim. Kamren had a few strawberry candles lit while sipping her Pink Blush Andre wine. She called Brody three times in the hour, but he didn't answer. She knew he was doing something he shouldn't been doing. This time, she wasn't going to panic or worry herself. If something was wrong, she would get a phone call or see it live on Channel 10 news.

Knock! Knock! Knock!

Kamren tossed her head backwards and shouted, "who is it?"

"It's Val, Kamren."

"Okay, give me a second," Kamren took a sip of her wine and stood to her feet. As she walked to the door, she could hear Val sniffing. She could tell something had to be wrong. Kamren opened the door, but something caught her attention. Valerie was holding a big and colorful drink in her right hand. Mascara was running down her face and stained her sheer white blouse.

"What is that?" Kamren asked. Valerie walked inside and said, "this is one of Cree's new creations. It's called Jamaican Suicide or something like that."

"What's in it?"

"Shit, I don't know, don't make me tell a lie. It sure has me with a buzz already, girl. I'll be back at Crystal's in a few." Valerie took a big sip, then placed the drink on the table. She flopped on the couch and exhaled loudly.

"What's wrong with you?"

"Girl, I don't even know where to start. Before I start talking shit, is B here?" Valerie asked.

"No, he's somewhere doing God knows what. Give me a sip of that drink though."

"Go head." Valorie pointed at the drink and leaned against the fluffy pillow. Kamren grabbed the big clear glass and took a few sips. The pretty glass reminded her of a fish bowl.
"Crystal needs to go global with these drinks." Kamren laughed.

"I know, that girl is a fool with this." Valerie said.

"Now, tell me what's up, talk to me."

"It all started about a month ago, I think. I logged into Tyson's email by mistake and saw he was emailing some girl."

"By mistake?" Kamren tilted her head and her eyebrows rose. Valerie flared her nose and batted her eyes.

"Okay, okay, I logged in purposely. I had this gut feeling he was doing something. You know I went with my move and I'm glad I did." Valorie said.

"Fuckin' right, forever going with our move." Kamren laughed.

"He's been meeting up with her and going on dates. He's cheating on me, Kam, I can't believe him."

"Wwhhattt??"

"He said he wouldn't cheat on me again, and I actually believed his lying ass. Once a cheater is always a cheater." Valerie said.

"Not necessarily, Val, people can change. That's like saying all men cheat and all women are faithful. Did you catch him in the act with his pants down?"
"Kind of, but not with his pants down. This nigga came home at 5:00 am today. Then when I asked him where he was, he flipped out on me. He said I'm always jumping down his throat for every little

thing he does. Tyson had the nerve to say I'm insecure and maybe I'm the one cheating. He made it so damn obvious that he's cheating, trying to flip the script on me!! Tyson thinks because he has a little money, he's irreplaceable. Hhmm, he sure thought wrong. He better go, to the left, to the left." Valerie jumped to her feet and hopped to the left twice. Kamren burst into laughter and pulled Valerie to sit down.

"You are a mess, a hot mess. Girl, have a seat and finish telling me what happened."

"I'm serious, Kam, I gave Tyson the best of me! I gave his ass all of me and everything I had. I accepted him when he didn't have shit. I gave him time to get it together and I took him back when he cheated on me. Now, he's cheating on me, AGAIN," Valerie covered her face and began to cry. Kamren's smile faded away. She sat closer to Valerie and gave her a hug. She hated seeing her best friend like this, especially because of someone she dearly loved.

"Do you know, or know of, the girl he's cheating with?"

"No, but I googled her name and found her information. She's from Lawtell, a real cute brown skin chick. Her edges are thin, but she's cute though. She graduated from Southeastern Louisiana University. She has a degree in Psychology and she's a psychologist. She recently started a little party planning business, as well. I guess that's her little side hustle."

"How do you know all of this?" Kamren asked, with a curious look scribbled on her face. Right about now, Valerie was sounding like a real-life stalker.

"I found her on Facebook and Instagram. You'll be surprised at how much people put their business on social media. Monday, she attended Zumba at Cajun Fitness. Wednesday, she had a facial after work. Thursday, she had drinks at Chips with her a few of her sorority sisters. They came to Opelousas to visit her. Friday, for breakfast, she a plain biscuit with a medium mocha frappe."

"Uuumm, okay. So, now that you know her schedule, what are you going to do?"

"I'm leaving his ass, THAT'S what I'm going to do. He cheated on me before and like a fool I stayed. I be damn if I stick around for it again. I may not have a degree like little Elizabeth Smith, but I have a good heart. Tyson comes home to a spotless and clean home. Unless he says otherwise, there is always a hot and delicious meal on the table. He's bath water is ready, I rub his feet, I give him facials, and I give him backrubs. This is how he repays me for my good loving? Just last month, we talked about getting out of that apartment and buying a home together. He said he was ready for kids and to get married. He can keep all that shit and give it to his fat ass mama. She acts like she wants to fuck him sometimes!"

"What does his mom have to do with anything? I thought you two were getting along now."

"We were, until I called her to get her advice. This bitch told me that her son is a good catch and I shouldn't leave him. She told me I would be a fool to leave him."

"What?" Kamren asked, she was a little surprised Tyson's mom would say something like that. Patty was the total opposite. Patty told Kamren the truth, even when she didn't want to hear it.

"Yes, Kamren, I was ready to choke her fat ass out. She acts like her son is perfect and doesn't do anything. At first, she didn't believe me. I had to email her the proof and shut her up quick."

"Wow, I guess she thought Tyson was perfect." Kamren said.

"Hhmm, I showed her wrong. I never thought we would be back in this place. Tomorrow, I'm moving out, I'll go to my sister's home. That's not going to last long, so I'm going to look for an apartment or rental home."

"You know you can stay here. I'll clean the guestroom for you." She said.

"Thanks, girl, I appreciate it. Will you help me move my things out of the apartment?" Valerie asked.

"Yea, I'm off tomorrow. Do we have to take the treadmill too?" Kamren asked and laughed.

"Duh, that was a stupid question. You know I need my treadmill, but I'll put it in a storage."

"You can put it in the outhouse. I'll get Brody to put it in there." Kamren said.

"Thanks, girl, I owe you, big time."

You don't owe me anything, you're my girl. I'm sorry y'all had to end like this. I know how much you love him."

"Fuck it, it is what it was," Valerie sipped her drink and ripped her tears. Kamren turned around and grabbed the box of Kleenex. She handed it to Valerie, then she grabbed the bottle of wine. She refilled her cup and exhaled.

"What's wrong with you?" Valerie asked.
"You may be helping me move my things out of here!"

"What, is Brody cheating too? It must be something in the codeine!"

"NO, he isn't cheating, calm down." Kamren said.

"If he isn't cheating, what's the problem?" Val asked.

"I don't know how much longer I can deal with Brody and his lifestyle."

"What do you mean?" Valerie asked.

"Well it's no secret what Brody does, but it should be a secret. I'm getting tired of feeling unsafe and worrying about him. It doesn't matter how many guns are in the house, sometimes I don't feel safe. I still think of the what if's and who is out to get him. I don't what to leave him, but it's like Brody won't change anytime soon. I try to make him go to church, but that doesn't last. He promised he would go back to school, but that didn't happen yet. I love him, but he needs time alone. Brody can't love me unless he gets his life in order."

"What if he doesn't get it together? What if he doesn't get his life together in the time period you want?" Valerie asked.

"Then I'll continue to live my life without Brody. I love him, damn, I love his ass, but what am I supposed to do? Am I supposed to stay with him and not be happy?"

"No, you deserve to be happy. Can you really see yourself without B? You two have been together for a while! That is the only man you have ever been with. All those other relationships weren't serious like this." Valerie said.

"I know, but I'm tired of trying. Maybe one of those hood rats will enjoy taking my place."

"Don't give up that easy, Kamren. I know how much Brody loves you. Sometimes, men need time to get it together."

"Exactly, he can get himself together by himself. When I leave maybe he'll get it together fast."

"I think you need one of Crystal's special drinks, let's go."

"Hold on." Kamren reached behind her couch and removed her phone off the charger. She slipped her gold sandals on and stood to her feet. Valerie walked out of the house first and pressed the small button on her keypad. It was a chilly outside and she wanted to start the car.

Kamren stretched her hand outside and quickly pulled in back in. Then she walked over the closet and grabbed one of Brody's LSU hoodies.

As she walked out of the house and pulled the hoodie over her head and locked the door. Valerie was sitting in the car anxiously waiting to drive off. She even leaned over to open the door for Kamren.

"Damn, girl, you must be thirsty." Kamren laughed and got into the car. Valerie laughed and sped off. Kamren head jerked and she onto the seat. The locked eyes and laughed.

"My bad, Kam, my head is all over the place." She said.

"Get it together, baby, everything is going to be okay. I was thinking we should do something soon."

"Like what?" Valerie asked.

"Go to the movies or eat out. With our crazy work schedules, I only see you at work."

"That is true, but how about we go to Lake Charles? I'm feeling lucky and the blackjack table is calling my name." Valerie stopped at the stop sign and rubbed her hands together. She laughed and continued driving. Kamren rolled her eyes and tossed her head backwards. Valerie was slightly obsessed with the blackjack table. She would spend big money every time she stepped into a casino.

"Girl, I'm giving you an allowance. I don't have time pulling you away from that damn table."

"Okay, okay, I won't overdue it this time. If I win some big money, don't ask me to take you to dinner." Valerie joked.

"Heeyyyy, it doesn't have to be all that." Kamren laughed. As Valerie drove pass Crystal's shop, she stared at the building. Kamren knew this was a set up and Valerie had no intentions to go there.

"Where are we going, Val, and please don't tell me we're going to that girl's house?"

"I guess you know me well. I'm getting my answers tonight, Kamren, fuck the dumb shit."

"Valerie, no, turn this car around now!"

"Too late, we're already here. I'm not going to do anything, I just want to make sure he's here."

"Why?" Kamren asked.

"Because, Kamren, he's my man and I have the right to know his whereabouts."

The neighborhood she lived in was wooded and dark. It was perfect for what Valerie had in mind. She rushed to park her car in the bushes and jumped out. It was a little distance from the house, but she didn't care. From a distance, Kamren noticed Tyson's black Ford Fusion parked in the driveway, she knew everything was about to go downhill.

"Val, please tell me we aren't getting down." Kamren shouted, in a whisper, from the passenger side and her eyes followed Valerie as she walked to the truck of her car. Valerie ignored her and popped her trunk. She pulled out a medal bat and a flat head screw driver.

"Yep, we sure are here, I got something for his ass." Valerie began to run and charged towards his car. Kamren rushed to unbuckle her seatbelt and got out of the car. She ran behind Valerie and grabbed her forearm. That didn't stop Valerie from dragging Kamren along the way.

"What are you about to do?" Kamren asked.

"Bust the windows." She said.

"Don't bust the windows!"

"Why not? It's going to make me feel better." Valerie said.

"You're going to make too much noise!! Don't bring all that drama around this girl's house. He's your problem, not her, don't be stupid!! Come on now, V, you're smarter than that." Valerie thought about it for a moment, but her mind was made up. She handed Kamren her car keys and held the bat in the air.

"VALERIE!"

"Shut up, Kamren, you probably would do the same if you were in my shoes!"

"NO, I wouldn't, I would pack my shit and leave his ass. Do you see me running around town clowning with Brody?"

"No, but he isn't cheating on you. I love him, but look at what he's doing to me. He's probably in there fucking her. He thinks he's going to play with ME like this AND get away with it? He really is a clown, just like I thought." Valerie stood in front of Tyson's car and her fingers began to tingle. She didn't know what to start destroying first. The tires looked nice, but the windows held her attention to the fullest.

"You need to use your head and think, girl! What if he comes outside and flash on you? What if she calls the cops on you? Think about it, Val, you can get into some serious trouble. Let's not forget about tampering with your career." Valerie was so angry, but Kamren's words were true. Valerie loved being a nurse and doing something stupid like this, could get her license suspended. None of this was worth her career or good reputation.

"You're right, Kam, what am I doing? This is not me at all, it must be the drink."

"Yea, be the bigger person. It's his lost, not yours, this shit is juvenile."

"Oh, Tyson, you're killing me." The laughter coming from Tyson and Elizabeth sent Valerie in rage! She dragged the tip of the screw driver across Tyson's car. The squeaky noise made Kamren uncomfortable and nervous. She covered her ears and took a step back, just in case she had to run.

"I gave him five years, five good years, Kam. Fuck him and her, they better live happily ever after." Valerie opened her pocket knife and stabbed the driver's side tire six times. She slapped the tip of the bat into the back window and it cracked. She ran around the car twice with the knife dragging across the paint job. Tyson's black car now looked white because all the scratches. Kamren wanted to stop her, but she was scared Valerie would swing the back at her.

"V, come on, that's enough!"

"No, it isn't, he's going to feel my pain." Valerie jumped on the hood on the car with the bat in the air. Her heart was racing and she was sweating like a pig. She didn't realize how much of a workout this was going to be.

"NO, no, no, no, Valerie... Don't do that." Valerie ignored Kamren and slammed the bat into his front window. Kamren gasped and jump back, the window began to crack. Valerie slammed the bat again, and again. Suddenly, glass shattered everywhere! She bust all the tires until they started to deflate. Valerie stared at the car feeling like she accomplished something spectacular. Her pain was only gone temporarily, but that was good enough for her.

"Tyson, did you hear that?" Elizabeth asked.

"Yea, let's go outside and see what's going on." Tyson said.

"Oh shit, get in the bushes." Kamren grabbed the bat and pulled Valerie off the car with one arm. She pulled her into the bushes with one arm around the neck and covered her mouth. They stumbled into the bushes, almost falling into an ant pile. Kamren placed her hands over Valerie's mouth before she could scream. They quietly watched Elizabeth and Tyson run out of the house in a frantic. Valerie was right, Elizabeth was a cutie. Her slim figure looked amazing in her striped sweater dress. The girl was fully dressed and could still turn a man, and a straight woman, on.

"What the fuck?" Tyson stood in front of his damaged car with his hands over his head.

"OH MY GOD! What the hell happened?" Elizabeth slowly walked around the car and examined it. She gasped louder, and louder, at every scratch, broken window, and flat tire.

"Who could have done this? No one knows you're here, right?"

"No, not a single soul. Look at my car, man, its done!"

"What if it was Dad? Maybe he knew you were coming here."

"Dad, did she just say dad?" Kamren whispered to Valerie. With wide eyes, she nodded her head up and down. She was very tempted to jump out of the bushes and ask a few questions.

"Is that his sister?" Kamren asked.

"Girl, no, Tyson doesn't have sisters. What the hell is really going on here?"

"We need to call the cops, right now."

"Do you have your phone?" Tyson asked. Staring at his car only made matters worse. Tyson's chest grew bigger, and bigger, from his heavy breathing. He shouted and punched the half-broken window. Blood was oozing out of his hand and Elizabeth gasped.

"Tyson, your hand is bleeding." Elizabeth ran to Tyson and grabbed his man. He screamed out in pain. As the pain increased, he realized how stupid it was to punch the window. Elizabeth untied the sweater that was around her waist and wrapped his hand with is.

"We need to go in the house, now!" She shouted. She didn't give Tyson a chance to reply. She grabbed his by the other hand and made him walk into the house. A trail of blood followed his every step until they walked into the house and closed the door.

"Girl, let's go, before we get hurt, or go to jail." Kamren jumped to her feet and helped her to her feet. They ran to Valerie's car without looking back. They could still hear Tyson shouting because of the pain. That didn't stop them though, they got into her car and drove off.

***

Valerie laid across her bed in a hot pink silk robe and fuzzy house slippers. Her hair was freshly washed and wrapped in a big blue towel. She had to take a hot shower to clear her mind, but it didn't help much. She stared at the white walls in silence thinking. She was a little confused and frustrated with everything that happened three hours ago. She hadn't heard from Tyson yet, but she wasn't sure if that was a good or bad thing. At least it meant that he didn't call her screaming about damaging his car.

Once Elizabeth called Tyson her brother, and he didn't correct her, everything changed. That one word answered a lot of questions, but she still need Tyson to clarify everything. Before Tyson's name was clear of cheating, he needed to tell her everything.

Valerie began to fall asleep, but the sound of the door startled her.

"Babe." Tyson shouted, as he walked down the hall. He entered his bedroom and smiled at Valerie. He loved seeing her bare face and wet curly hair. He kicked his shoes off and walked to the bed. Valerie pointed at his hand and said, "hey, baby, what happened to your hand?" From the tip of his finger, to his wrist, was wrapped with white bandage. Majority of the bandage was stain with blood and looked disgusting. Valerie was ready to unwrap it and be the nurse she is.

"It's a long story and I'm trying to figure out where to start."

"Okay, but I didn't hear your car. Where did you park?" She asked.

"I was dropped here, you won't believe what I'm about to tell you." Tyson shook his head and got into bed. He rubbed his eyes and yawned. He was slightly tired, but he needed to talk to Valerie.

"What happened?" She asked.

"I'll start from the beginning, bear with me. A few weeks ago, a girl wrote me on Facebook. She said we needed to talk about something important, but I ignored her. Two days after that, I receive an email from the same girl. She started telling me how her mom told her about her real father."
"What?" She asked.

"Just listen, the man her mother is referring to, is my dad."

"WHAT, ARE YOU SERIOUS, TYSON?" Valerie stood on in the bed and sat on her knees. What they heard was right and she needed more details.

"I wish I was lying, but I'm not. Elizabeth and I are six months apart. My dad had an affair with her mom back in the day. When she told him she was pregnant, he begged her to have an abortion. She didn't want to have an abortion, so he started threatening her. He would drive pass her house all the time. Leave crazy voicemails on her phone and even stalked her. It got to the point that she began scared and got a restraining order on him. They moved to Hammond and never looked back. The man that her mom is married to now is the man she thought was her father."

"This is crazy, Tyson, it sounds like a Lifetime movie. What made her mom tell her after all these years?" Valerie asked.

"She said because she couldn't hold the secret in any longer. For years, it bothered her, and it was time to come clean. For thirty-four years, that lady held that secret in, that's crazy." Tyson said.

"This is... I want to say crazy, but crazy is an understatement. All this time, I thought your only siblings were Alfred and Matthew, not some random girl from Hammond. How could he a keep a secret like this from your mom? Are you going to tell her what happened?"

"Yea, I have to, I can't keep this away from her. The family needs to know her and the truth."

"What if they have a problem with her? That might run her away and she'll never come back."

"Then they'll have a problem with me. It isn't her fault what happened, she's the victim in all this. Elizabeth reminds me a lot of you, I hope you two get along."

"She does, really?"

"Yea." Tyson said.

"I'm one of a kind, so I would love to hear how." Valerie pointed to the bed and made Tyson sit down. He held his hand and slowly sat on the bed. He turned to Valerie and gave her a kiss and said, "she's ambitious, smart, funny, and kind. I really want you two to meet and get along. I'm thinking about inviting her and her boyfriend over for dinner next week. You can cook your famous shrimp stew and cornbread." He smiled.

"With my homemade lemonade and pecan pie for dessert. I can't wake to meet her, baby. It seems like you two are getting along well."

"We are, and you can tell she's my sister. I overheard her on the phone with her boyfriend. That girl exposed on him in a matter of seconds." He laughed.

"That sounds a lot like you in the past weeks," Valerie rolled her eyes and nudged Tyson on the shoulder. He grabbed her hand and covered it with kisses. She wanted to be upset with him, but she couldn't. Tyson was dealing with a lot and she needed to cut him some slack.

"I know and I'm sorry, sweetheart. All this mess with my sister drove me crazy. All my life, I looked up to my dad, until now. This is foul, and he has to answer for it, he won't get away with it. My mom is a damn good woman to him and he does something like this to her? I could never look at him same again."

"I don't blame you, Tyson, things are going to be crazy with the truth comes out."

"Hell yea, and I'm ready for it. No one will disrespect my mom and sister, NO ONE!"

"Awww, look at you being a big brother to your secret sister. I'm proud of you, baby." Valerie grabbed Tyson's face and kissed him.

"I'm trying, baby, she deserves to know her real family." He said.

"She does and I'm glad you're helping her through this process. Is she scared, I know I would be?"

"Yea, she is, she's scared of everyone's reaction. Especially my dad's reaction, no telling what he's going to say."

"I hope this doesn't start a fight between anyone." She said.

"I don't mind body slamming anyone on the kitchen table." He laughed.

"Oh Lord, Tyson, don't take it to that level. Keep your hands and all objects to yourself. You're trying to resolve a situation, not add fuel to it."

"No one better start shit with us. I'm making things right and they better respect that." Tyson said.

"So how does all of this fit into what happened to your car?" She asked.

"I'm not sure, but I wish I knew. Elizabeth and I were talking, when we heard a loud bang. When we ran outside, we didn't see anyone. My tires were on a flat, my car was keyed, and the windows were busted. I got so mad, I punched the window and cut my hand."

"That was stupid." She laughed.

"It was stupid of me to do that. Elizabeth made me to go to the hospital to check on it. I have six stitches and a prescription for some pain medicine. I'm sorry I didn't call you and tell you to come to the hospital. I wanted to tell you all this in private."

"It's okay, baby, I forgive you. Enough of that, I want to talk about this dick being in my mouth." She smiled and laughed. She tucked her loose hair behind her big ears and reached for the rubber that was on her dresser. Valerie pulled her long hair into a tight ponytail and tugged it a little. She wanted to make sure her ponytail was tight and secured.

"Oh yea, it shouldn't be much talking, do you, red." Tyson grabbed the back of Valerie's head and pulled her closer to him. They passionately kissed one another as if it was their first kiss. He ran his fingers through her hair and grabbed her bare ass. She unbuckled his belt and maneuvered his white denim Levi's to his knees. By using his other foot, he wiggled the jeans off and they fell to the floor.

Valerie climbed on top of Tyson and grind against his penis. The tingling sensation they both were feeling felt amazing. She grabbed his index finger and shoved it into her vagina. Her warm pussy made his dick jump. The way he moved his fingers in her pussy, made her moan loudly. She pulled his finger out of vagina and put it in her mouth. The clear substance was sticky and sweet. She licked his fingers until her juices were gone.

"Damn, girl, I love when you do that shit. How does my pussy taste?" He asked.

"It tastes good, daddy, just like you like it." Valerie rubbed her lips against his so he could taste her pussy.

Tyson was turned on so much, he grabbed her breasts, and started to nibble on them. Tyson suddenly stopped, the fourplay wasn't enough. He was ready to fuck his girlfriend like she was ugly.

**

Kamren sat in her living room, sipping on a new bottle of wine. After experiencing the drama she just did, she was sipping her wine, straight out of the bottle. She wanted to call Valerie and check her, but she decided not to. Eventually, Valerie would call her and spill the news.

Brody still wasn't home, and she hadn't spoken to him yet. This time, she wasn't going to panic. She hadn't received numerous phone calls about a murder or death. Therefore, she was okay and calm.

Five minutes later, her phone rang, it was Valerie. She quickly placed the bottom on the table and answered the phone.

"Hello?" Kamren said.

"Hey, girl, are you busy?" Valerie asked.

"No, not at all, still sipping. What's up with you?"

"Making a nice ole turkey sandwich, Tyson finally came home. You won't believe what Tyson told me!!"

"Girl, what? Tell me!"

"Indeed, Elizabeth is his sister. That's why she called him her brother." Valerie stepped out of the kitchen and stood at the end of the hall. She wanted to make sure he was still sleeping. She smiled when she heard he was snoring loudly.

"Hell no, how, when? I need answers!"

"I'm going to make this long ass story short. Elizabeth's mom told her the truth. The man that she's married to now, she had Elizabeth thinking that he was her father. Elizabeth and Tyson are six months apart. Their dad wanted her to have an abortion, but she didn't. He became so crazy, but she had to get a restraining order. She moved to Hammond and forgot all about him. She got tired of keeping it a secret, so she told her. Now, Elizabeth and Tyson are ready to tell his mom."

"Girrrllllll, that's a story for you. Who would have thought his dad would be no good like that?"
"No one, and especially Tyson. They want to tell his mom everything."

"Really, when?" Kamren asked.

"They want to tell her Friday, but I want you to come with us."

"What, are you sure about this? This seems like a family affair and I don't think I should a part of it."

"Girl, cut it out, you are family. Do you think the same blood or last name to make us closer? Besides, if shit goes left, we're going to need you to calm it down." She laughed.

"I guess here, I'll come, but if a fight breaks out, I am not stopping it. I can't afford to get hit in the face." She laughed.

"Hopefully, everyone keeps their hands to themselves. If not, Tyson will shut it down quick. He's waiting for his dad to get out of line."

"Oh Lord, I'm going to need tennis shoes." She laughed.

"Where is Brody, I don't hear his loud mouth?"

"That's because his loud ass still isn't home." Kamren said.

"Brody isn't home and you aren't worried? Wow, I guess you are serious about all this." Valerie said.

"I am, I need some peace of mind. I love him, but Brody won't be the death of me. I'm too young to die of a stroke or heart attack." She laughed.

"I hear you, girl, and I don't blame you for feeling that way."

"Did Tyson say anything about his car?" Kamren asked.

"Not really and I'm not a suspect. That's a win, win, for me." A bright light flashed on the house and it made

Kamren nervous. She reached under the couch for the .45 and ran to the window. She slightly peeked out of the window, then she exhaled. It was only Brody, and she was happy. She ran back to the couch and tucked the gun. Seconds later, Brody walked into the house yawning.

"Brody just walked in, I'll call you tomorrow." Kamren said.

"Okay, bye." Kamren disconnected the call and walked to the door. She purposely gave him a hug, so she could smell his shirt. It didn't linger of marijuana and she smiled. That meant Brody's eyes were red because he was tired and not high.

"Hey, baby, I have a story for you." She laughed.

"What's up?" Brody kicked his Air Force Ones off, and they walked into the living room. Brody sat on the couch and he pulled Kamren to sit next to him. He pulled her legs onto her lap and began to rub her feet. The foot rub felt so good, she forgot what she wanted to say.

"Tonight, we found out that Tyson has a sister and they are six months apart."

"Huh?"

"That was my same reaction. Shit was crazy last night, I don't even know where to start."

Chapter 5 February 2012

Elizabeth, Tyson, Valerie, and Kamren, sat in rental car in front of his parent's house. Today, everyone was home, including his brothers. Kamren was calm, but she could hear everyone's hearts beating. She rubbed Valerie's shoulder and said, "everyone needs to calm down, we're not going to war or rob a bank."

"It's a possibility that this can turn into a war. You know my dad hates when his shit is put on front street. He might flip out when he sees Elizabeth." Tyson said.

"He probably won't recognize her." Kamren said.

"It would be hard not to, her and Tyson are practically twins." Valerie said.

"You are right about that, Elizabeth looks like Tyson with a wig on." Kamren laughed.

"At least I know I would be a pretty girl." He laughed.

"Tyson, are you sure we should do this?" Elizabeth stared at the house and tapped her fingernails against the window. She was sweaty under her arms and scent was slowly increasing. Elizabeth opened her shirt and fanned her underarms. She was too nervous and ready to run away.

"Yea, I'm sure, it's time to let the truth be told. Are you backing out?" Tyson asked.

"A little, I'm scared of how everyone is going to react to me."

"I thought you wanted to do this? You came this for, let's go all the way." Tyson said.

"Stop worrying yourself, Elizabeth, if anyone says something crazy, Tyson will punch them in the face." Valerie laughed.

"Especially Alfred, he still owes me $125 for the car part." Tyson said.

"I have to be to work in an hour, so let's do this," Kamren clapped her hands and opened the door. Everyone else got out of the car and closed their doors. Tyson felt his heart drop, but he played it cool. He didn't want the women to see him panic. He knew his dad had an ugly side, but Valerie and Kamren didn't know that. When he was eleven years old, he saw his dad slam his mom into the wall. She pretended it didn't happen, even when Tyson confronted her about it. Since that day, he always looked at his dad a little different.

"You're right, maybe I'm overreacting."

"I got you, don't worry about anything." Tyson said.

"Do you promise?" She asked.

"Yes, I promise, now let's go inside." Tyson grabbed his sister by the hand and lead her to the house. Everyone stood at the door and waited for Tyson to knock.

"It's me, Mom." Tyson shouted.

"Come in, baby, the door is open." Tyson opened the door and motioned for everyone to follow behind him. Elise and Dennis were standing in the kitchen cooking. As she stirred the pot, Dennis kissed her neck, and held her hips. After all the years they were together, they never lost the spark or fire in their marriage.

Alfred and Matthew sat in the living room watching the cooking channel. Next year, they were planning to open a small bakery. They often watched the cooking channel to get ideas and inspiration.

"What's up, everyone?" Tyson closed the door and clapped his hands together. The loud noise grabbed his brothers and parent's attention. Elise dropped her oven mitt on the countertop and smiled.

"Tyson, what are you doing here?" Elise walked to Tyson and gave him a hug. Then she smiled at Kamren and Valerie and gave them a hug. She didn't know who Elizabeth was, but she gave her a hug also. Elise was a friendly woman and showed everyone genuine love.

"Valerie, who's your new friend?" She asked. Dennis stared at Elizabeth, and he knew exactly who she was. The shocked look on his face was priceless. His face was flushed, Tyson could see his father's hands were shaking.

Elizabeth stood behind Tyson, but he grabbed her hand, and made her stand next to him. He wanted to show her he honestly had her back.

"Uumm, Tyson, you should answer this question." Valerie smiled, without showing teeth, and stood behind Tyson.

"Uumm-" Dennis tried to speak, but he couldn't gather a decent sentence.

"Dad, do you want to tell Ma who she is?" Tyson asked.

"Why would your dad want to tell me who your friend is? Tyson and Dennis, what's going on? Is there something I don't know about, but I need to know about?"

"Yea, Mom, there is." Tyson said.

"Baby, this is-"

"I'm Elizabeth and I'm your step daughter. It's nice to finally meet you. Since I met Tyson, he's said great things about you."

"What?" Matthew and Alfred shouted and jumped to their feet. Dennis dropped his head and turned away. Elizabeth tried to shake Elise's hand, but she pulled away. Tyson was shocked, that was his first time seeing his mom be rude to anyone.

"How do you know for sure this is your daughter, Dennis?" Elise asked.

"We did a DNA test, Mom, and it proves it," Tyson reached into his back pocket and held the paper in the air. She snatched the paper out of his hand and quickly unfolded it. She read the results and crumbled the paper.

"What?" Elise shouted. She turned around to look at her husband, but he was too shame and guilty to look at her. Alfred and Matthew ran into the kitchen. They stared at Elizabeth, then glanced at Tyson. All the siblings could see the resemblance in one another.

"Dad, is this true?" Alfred asked. Dennis raised his head and nodded it up and down. Alfred, Elise, and Matthew, gasped. Dennis closed his eyes and clenched his fist. His family's reaction to the news made him feel like a piece of shit.

"I want to hear it from your mouth, Dennis. Who is this young lady and how do you know her?" Elise's skin was boiling like water. Words couldn't explain how hurt and angry she was feeling right now.

"This young lady is my daughter, Elizabeth Scott. I know her, well, because she IS my daughter. Her and Tyson are close in age." He said.

"Hhhmmm, how close in age are they?" She asked.

"Like six months apart, close in age." Tyson said. The three gasped again, but this time, started to cry. In that moment, she wanted to hate Elizabeth, but heart wouldn't allow her to.

"Why did you do this, Tyson, why are you causing so much confusion??"

"Me?"

"I found Tyson and reached out to him. Not the other way around." Elizabeth said.

"Elizabeth, just stay out of this, this is family business." Dennis shouted.

"What do you mean, family business? I am family, Dad, even if you don't want to admit it."

"This is not her fault, Dad, and you know it. For over thirty years you hid this secret. All of this is your fault and you know it."

"I'm sorry, Mrs. Elise, I didn't come here to start any confusion. I just wanted to meet my real family. My entire life has been a lie. My mom told me someone else was my dad. I just wanted the truth and some answers. I'm sorry I even came here and disturbed your family. Goodbye, everyone, and have a nice life." Elizabeth ran to the door in tears, but Kamren chased behind her. She blocked the door and grabbed Elizabeth's hand. Then she grabbed her by the shoulders and made her turn around. She didn't want anyone to see her crying, so she turned away.

"Now wait a minute everyone! If anyone is going to play the blame game, it sure isn't Mr. Dennis. Elizabeth did what was right and what her heart allowed her to do. How dare you, Mr. Dennis? I thought you were better than this. Clearly, you're not, this is your mess. You need to clean it up and accept the responsible for your actions. Just imagine how Elizabeth felt the moment her mom told her the truth. All the lies replayed in her head and nothing made sense anymore."

"This is none of your business, Kamren, so stay out of it!" Dennis shouted.

"Frankly, I don't care whose business this is. Clearly, you weren't taking care of YOUR business, because you got another woman pregnant."

"You better watch your damn mouth in my home. You have no right sticking your nose into family business, little girl."

"I'm a grown ass woman. See, Valerie, this is why I didn't want to come here. I don't have time for this shit, I have my own issues. I'll be in the car waiting for y'all," Kamren raced to the door and rushed out. She slammed the heavy door, making everyone jump. Kamren's words were harsh, but it didn't take anyone's mind off the real subject.

"Dad, how could you do this to Mom?" Alfred asked. His tone of voice showed that pain was filling his body. He stared at his dad, then he stared at Elizabeth. He didn't know what to say or do anymore.

"If her and Tyson are six months apart, that means you cheated on Mom. Dad, did you cheat on mom with some random woman?" Matthew asked.

"Excuse, my mom wasn't just some random woman. They were dating for a year, but I guess no one knew about that part."

"Your mom was my mistress!"

"MY MOM WAS YOUR GIRLFRIEND! I know it was a long time ago, but let's not play dumb. I saw the letters and the pictures. You had plans to marry her. You wanted to travel places with her, so don't front in front of your wife. You were real cozy with your 'mistress.'

Elise walked into the kitchen and stood in front of her husband. He could barely look her in the eyes without feeling disappointed in himself.

"How could you do this to me, your kids, and your family?" Elise raised her hand in the air and slammed it against her husband's face. Elizabeth and Valerie gasped, and held onto each other.

"It was a mistake!" He shouted.

"What part was a mistake? Was it sleeping with another woman, or getting her pregnant? WHAT IS, DENNIS? BECAUSE I NEED ANSWERS!!!"

"Getting her pregnant was a mistake, but having a relationship with her wasn't. That's the truth, since you wanted it. At the time, I loved her, but I met you, all that changed."

"Did you know she was pregnant?" Alfred asked.

"Yes, I did, but I didn't want her to keep it."

"Tell them rest, this is the best part." Elizabeth said.

"He threatened her to have an abortion, and when she didn't, things got ugly. He started to threaten and stalk her. He did it so much, she ran off to Hammond." Tyson said.

"Wow, who are you? In a matter of minutes, you have become an unknown person." Elise said.

"I am not an unknown person!!
I am your husband, the same man that
loves you. We've been married for
over twenty years, you know me,
Elise."

"No, I don't know you. How
could you do this, that's my only
question?"

"I was young and stupid, Elise!
I wasn't thinking, and I'm sorry, once
again. Are you going to let this ruin
our marriage?"

"I don't want to talk about this
anymore. I'll be back later or
whenever." Dennis tried to stop Elise,
but she pulled her arm away. Elise
grabbed her purse and ran out of the
house. Elizabeth and Dennis locked
eyes, but he charged her way. Before
anyone saw it coming, Dennis grabbed
Elizabeth by the neck and slammed her
into the wall. She tried to fight him off,
but his grip was tight around her neck.
Alfred his father by the neck and threw
him on the ground.

"Dad, what the fuck is wrong
with you? You told us never put our
hands on a woman? Are you fucking
crazy?" Tyson attacked his dad by
getting on top of him and putting his
hands around his throat. Dennis buried
his bald fingernail tips into Tyson's
neck. He gasped for air, but he couldn't
inhale much. Alfred pulled his dad by

the shoulders, and Matthew pulled Tyson by the waistline.

"Tyson, stop, he's turning purple." Valerie shouted from a distance. She wasn't foolish enough to stop Tyson while he was in rage. He was liable to push her away, but not mean any harm.

"Everyone, stop it, just stop it," Elizabeth screamed, and jumped up and down. Her tears and sobbing didn't stop anyone. Kamren ran into the house and ran to Tyson. Once she saw what was going on, she tackled Tyson to the floor. Valerie was shocked that she was able to get him flat on the floor.

"Bro, calm down!" Alfred shouted. Matthew held Tyson's wrists, and pinned them to the ground. Tyson tried fighting back, but he was too tired. Sweat was forming on his face and his body became weak. He inhaled and exhaled several times.

Dennis rubbed his neck and stumbled to the kitchen table. He grabbed his car keys and ran out of the house. Everyone was going crazy in the house, but no one said anything. Valerie ran to Tyson and he was breathing heavily. She kissed his sweaty forehead and stood him to his feet.

"Let's go, everyone, NOW," Kamren banged on the wall and pointed to the door. Like little soldiers, everyone followed behind Kamren. She turned around and shoved her hands into Tyson's pockets. Kamren grabbed the keys, and everyone got into the car.

"What the fuck happened?" Kamren asked. She started the car and drove off. No one answered her, so she asked the question again.

"His mouth is what happened, Kamren. This is his mess and he had the nerve to blame it on everyone else!" Valerie said.

"I need to find my mom, I need to find her now," Tyson looked up and down the Frontage Road, but his mom's red Malibu was nowhere in sight. He banged on the dashboard, but he slightly startled Kamren. She swerved a little, but quickly gathered herself and pulled to the shoulder of the road. Everyone was on ten and needed to calm down.

Kamren turned the car off and said, "look, everyone, we need to calm down."

"I need to find my mom!"

"Okay, try calling her phone." Kamren said.

"She doesn't have it. It was on the table when we left." He said.

"Damn, what about your dad? Never mind, that was a stupid question. Have your mom ever left like this before?"

"I can't recall, it's been a long time I've seen everyone get angry like this."

"I should have never found you. I started this entire mess and your mom and dad will hate me forever," Elizabeth turned away and stared out of the window. She couldn't wait to get in her car and go home. She would speak to Tyson, or anyone in his family, again.

"No, it isn't, so stop saying that." Valerie said.

Tyson began to think and within

seconds, a smile appeared on his face.

"Go to the hospital!"

"Which hospital, this one right here?" Kamren pointed at the hospital that was up the road. Tyson nodded his head and Kamren turned the car.

Once again, his heart was pounding out of his chest and he was nervous.

"Why the hospital, baby?"

"Years ago, my mom and dad got into an argument. She left for three hours and no one knew where she was, and she wasn't answering her phone. When she came home, my dad asked her where she. She said she was at the hospital looking at the babies. My dad asked her why she is still doing that, and she started shouting at him. My dad stopped the conversation and made us go outside. We never knew why, but it didn't bother me."

"Well, maybe she's here, and you can find out. It seems like your family has a few secrets in the closet." Valerie said.

"A few too many secrets in our family closet."

***

Elise leaned against the window, silently crying. Her eyes were glossy, baggy, and red. Her hands were pressed against the glass and she stared at the newborn babies. Some was Caucasian, some was African American, and a few were Asian. The all seemed peaceful and innocent. If they only knew what this dirty world could do to them, they wouldn't want to grow up. They would stay babies forever and never leave their parent or parents' side.

Tyson stood mid-way in the quiet hall, staring at his mom. She knew he was standing behind her, but didn't say anything.

"Mom." Tyson whispered.

"Yes?" She asked.

"A-ar-are you okay, Mommy? I was worried sick about you." Tyson said.

"I'm okay, baby, and thank you for being concerned about your mother. It doesn't surprise me that you were the one who came."

"Of course, I was coming to look for you. I'm your favorite son, and you're my favorite girl." He smiled.

"Yes, always, and forever, my sweet, baby boy. I'm surprised you found me here. Did you tell your father I'm here? He probably would have a heart attack if he knew I was here." Elise used her jacket's sleeve to wipe her wet face and laughed in a fake way.

"No, I didn't tell him, things got crazy when you left." Tyson said.

"That doesn't surprise me, at all. Where is your crew?" She asked.

"They stayed in the car. I wanted to talk to you alone and get some answers."

"I'm pretty sure your sister wants some answers also."

"Yea, she does, but I need to talk to you first." Tyson said.

"How did you know I was here?" She asked.

"This might sound crazy, but I thought about something from the past. When I was a kid, you and dad got into an argument. When you came home, he asked you where you were, but it seemed like he already knew where you were. You didn't exactly say where you were, but your context clues were enough. Why do you always come here, Mom? What's so special about staring at a bunch of babies you don't know?" Tyson asked.

"You would be surprised at the how much kids listen. You have a great memory, I like that."

"Mom, you still haven't said why do you come here." Tyson sighed.

"I come here because I imagine my baby being here. I stare at the babies and think about which baby my baby would look like. Would it have this or that? Would it be a girl or a boy? The questions are endless, I could do this for days." She chuckled.

"When were you pregnant, Mom, did you have a miscarriage?" Tyson asked.

"Your dad and I was so hot and horny, I got pregnant eight weeks after you were born. I didn't know how to tell my parents, so Dennis did. Your grandmother called us all kinds of nasty freaks. We didn't get mad, we just laughed. About three months into my pregnancy, your father started getting stressed out about the baby. He said we couldn't afford another baby and I had to get an abortion. I cried for days, but that didn't change your father's decision. We weren't rich, but I felt like we had money for a second baby. Having that abortion was my biggest regret. Now that I look back at it, I should have left your father then. Of course, I didn't, I was young and in love. Then, a few months after that, I get a phone calls from some woman. She said it was about my husband and she needed to speak to me. I met her at the Shell gas station on Creswel Lane. I'll never forget that day, I swear. It was cold, gloomy, and raining. Before I could ask her if my husband was okay, she hands me a folder. It was full of papers." Elise said.

"What were the papers?" Tyson asked.

"She had pictures, phone records, and emails of her and your father. The last paper was an ultrasound. Elizabeth isn't your only sister," Elise covered her face with her shirt and sobbed. She was embarrassed at her own words, even though it wasn't her secret. She was only a part of the secret.

"MOM, WHAT?" Yet again, Tyson was confused. Elise reached into her pocket and pulled out a folded piece of paper. She handed it to Tyson and said, "take this," without reply, Tyson reached for the paper and opened it. It had the name Joe'Ann Chenier written in big letters. Underneath, in a smaller font, said Mary Ann Street, Opelousas Louisiana.

Tyson read the address and name three times, but it didn't make sense. He handed his mom the paper, but she pushed his hand towards his pocket.

"No, baby, you need that."

"Mom, what is going on?" He asked.

"You have another sister and her name is Joe' Ann Chenier. I'm not sure what's the full address, I haven't spoken her in a year. You, her, and Elizabeth, are all six months a part. No, I'm sorry, she's seven months apart from you two."

"Wait a minute, wait a minute, wait a damn minute! You know about this Joe' Ann person and never said anything??"

"Yes, and I made him choose the baby or me. I told him he wasn't claiming a child that didn't come out of my vagina. He happy I told him that and I knew it. It's not he tried to reach out to her. Once I matured and became a woman, I had to reach out to her. When your father found out I was communicating with her, we got into a huge argument. I'm so ashamed of myself for putting that little girl through that. Because of my dumb ass, she didn't grow up without a father. At the time, I was so angry, Tyson! Your father made ME have an abortion, because he had another woman pregnant. Little did I know, he actually had three women pregnant."

"Dad did all of that, I can't believe this. All of this have to be a lie, Mom. Dad has his ugly ways, but this doesn't sound like Dad." Tyson said.

"Trust me, if you knew your father back then, you wouldn't be surprised." Elise said.

"If you knew about her, that means you knew about Elizabeth this entire time." Tyson said.

"No, I knew NOTHING about Elizabeth. I was just as shocked just as everyone else. Joe'Ann, on the other hand, I did know about that. I know you have a lot of questions and I'm going to try and answer as many as I can. You have to promise me something, Tyson." Elise said.

"What's that, Mom? How I'm feeling about you right now, you shouldn't ask me for much."

"Tyson, I don't care how angry or hurt you are. You will NOT disrespect me, you are my son, and I'm your mother. You aren't too old for me to lay your ass out. Do you hear me, boy, don't let that little hair on your chest and chin get to you. I may be saved, but the girl from the projects is itching to give you AND your father an L. You got that, did I make myself loud and clear?"

"Yes... Ma'am... I hear you, loud and clear."

"Like I was saying, you have to promise me something." Elise said.

"Anyways, Mom, what is it?" Tyson walked to his mom and gave her a hug. She padded his head and rubbed his back. Since Tyson was the youngest boy, he was a mama's boy. When Tyson was younger, you couldn't pay him to leave his mom's side. His dad and brothers always teased him about it. He didn't care at all. His mom was always an upbeat and joyful woman, he loved being in her presence.

"You have to promise me that you won't judge me. Just like your father has a past, I also have one also. No, it's not full of grimy streets stories, but they are terrible. I was a weak woman. And I allowed your father to walk all over me. Your father literally, treated me like a doormat. Why did I allow it? Because I loved him, and I didn't want to see another woman with him. I look at everything now, and it wasn't worth it. NONE OF it was worth it, and I wish I could take it all back. Neither one of those girls deserved what your father and I put them through."

"You and Dad really hurt Elizabeth today, Mom."

"I need to speak to her one on one. I'm not upset with her, I would have done the same thing. She has the right to want to know her family. I know she has plenty of questions and I'll answer as many as I can. Your father can be an evil man and I'm not sure if he would talk to her."

"How could you be with a man like that, Mom?" Tyson asked.

"I don't know, Tyson, I'm asking myself that question now. I'm not sure that I can be with your father anymore. I'm tired and all cried out."

***

Kamren arrived at the Cotton's residence in a panic. The phone call she received from Patty made her a nervous wreck. She left from work and went straight to the Cotton's home. She didn't care about the red lights, yield signs, and stop signs, she ignored along the way. She needed to make it there fast and figure out what was going on.

Patty didn't give Kamren any details on the phone. The only thing she cried out was. "My baby, my baby, not my sweet baby, my baby is dead!" Patty's words made Kamren's heart ache and she couldn't control her tears. What made matters worse, Brody wasn't answering her calls. She knew something had to be wrong with him.

Valerie parked next to Kamren's car and rushed out of her car. She didn't care about taking her keys out of the ignition or grabbing her purse. She followed behind Kamren, but she didn't say anything. She wasn't sure what to say because she didn't know what was going on.

Kamren opened the door and found everyone in the living room crying. She was surprised to see some of Brody's relative here that she hadn't see in months. A few arguments and disagreement had them staying their distant from one another.

"Mrs. Patty... What happened to Brody? Where is Brody, and please, tell he isn't dead. You can tell me he's hurt, but PLEASSSEE, Mrs. Patty, don't tell me he's dead. Don't tell me someone killed my boyfriend," Kamren's lips trembled, plus, her legs started to shake. She covered her mouth and leaned against the door. The feeling of butterflies floating in her stomach took over. It wasn't a good feeling and she couldn't control it at all. She almost fell to the floor, but Valerie was there to catch her.

"No, Kamren, it isn't Brody," Patty turned to her husband and cried harder. Brody Junior tried to fight back his tears, but he couldn't. He grabbed the back of his wife's head and buried her chest into his chest. They slowly fell to the floor and cried together. Whatever pain they were feeling, Kamren could feel it as well. It felt a cold and irritated feeling through her body.

No one wanted to tell her anything and she was seconds from losing her mind. She ran to Brody's older cousin, Ashlee, who was crying. Kamren grabbed her by the face and asked, "Ash, what is wrong, tell me something!!! Is it Brody, I need to know!"

"It isn't B, he's, he's, he's in Natasha's room."

"Okay, so what's wrong?" She asked.

"It's Natasha, Kamren, she's dead." Ashlee cried out. She wiped her runny nose with her hand and wiped it on her plain t-shirt. Kamren shouted, "WHAT?"

"Oh my God, no!" Valerie gasped and whispered.

"She accidentally drowned at the pool party. Some little boy thought she was joking when she said she couldn't swim. He pushed her into the pool and she freaked out. One of the parent's tried to save her, but he couldn't. It was too late, and now, she's dead." Ashlee's tears grew bigger and she collapsed into Kamren's arms. Kamren could feel her entire world crashing by the second. Her and Ashlee stumbled to the floor and her body went numb.

"Please tell me you're lying, Ashlee, this can't be real," Kamren whispered, as she rocked side to side. She tried comforting Ashlee, but she needed some to comfort her as well.

"It's okay, Kamren, everything is going to be okay." Valerie felt bad for lying to Kamren, but she didn't know what to say. She wasn't sure how she could stop her friend from hurting, but she was in pain as well. Being friends with Kamren made her close with Brody's family. She also looked at Natasha as her little sister.

A few moments later, Brody walked out of Natasha's room with a bear in his hand. Kamren locked eyes with Brody and crawled his way. She stood to her feet and sobbed.

Brody punched the wall and burst into tears. Kamren was startled, but she still managed to hug Brody. No one said anything, they cried together.

"Why, why?" Brody whimpered, in a way Kamren never heard before. With every tear that fell on her shoulder, she held him tighter.

"Brody, it's okay, I'm here for you."

"It's not okay, how did I let this happen? I was supposed to protect her, Kamren. I'm always supposed to protect her," Brody jumped to his feet and sent several holes into the walls. Everyone was startled by his rage.

"Brody, calm down." Kamren demanded, but he ignored her. He was so emotional, he didn't know what to do with himself. He could literally, feel his heart crumbling in pieces and it wasn't a good feeling.

***

Brody sat outside with a dry stream of tears on his cheeks. A pack of Newport cigarettes were on his left side and a bottle of whiskey was to the left. Natasha's bear was on his lap, but a blank stare was sitting on his face. He held the bear tight and he couldn't let it go. It was very special to Natasha, simply because of Brody. Last May, they attended the Cajun Heart Land State Fair all week. On the third day, Natasha spotted the bear and fell in love with it. Brody played basketball for an hour to win the bear. He wasn't great in basketball, but that day he was. The bear was baby blue, with a red nose, and tan paws. The middle of the bear had a white patch that said *I Love You*. Every time he stared at the bear, a little piece of life left him. Now he knew what it felt like to be empty. The pain he was feeling, no would understood.

He sat outside for hours, thinking and crying. He thought about how Natasha died, the way she screamed for her life, the way she fought for her life, and more. Brody felt guilty and that he should have been the one to die. In his eyes, everyone blamed him for Natasha's death.

Kamren slowly walked outside and leaned against the door. She stood in the bathroom for twenty minutes crying, but she had to pull herself together. She needed to check on Brody and make sure he wasn't losing his mind. She tried everything she could to wash his guilt away, but she couldn't.

"Baby, please come inside. It's cold, it's midnight, and the rain is coming soon." Kamren was wearing UGG Boots, gym shorts, and a long sleeve cropped top. She was shivering, but Brody was worth it.

"She should have been with me, Kamren. We were supposed to be at the movies, eating popcorn, and laughing our asses off at some silly movie. She would ask me to buy her everything on the menu, and I would have. Then her stomach would be been in pain, and my mom would have blamed it on me. It was our routine and we did this every Saturday. I messed it up, I cancelled our plans and I can't fix it, Kamren. I don't know what to do with myself, I'm going crazy!! Help me, baby, I don't to lose my mind," Brody cried, in a high pitch, and pulled his knees to his chest.

Before Kamren approached him, she wiped away her tears. She had to find the strength to pull him together. She sat next to him and placed his head onto her shoulder. She held him with one hand and rubbed his shoulder. In the time she's been with Brody, she never heard him cry like this. She never witnessed him this emotional and destroyed.

"This is not your fault, and I will not allow you to say, or feel, this way. It's no one's fault, so no one can play the blame game. We all know Natasha was an angel who somehow escaped from Heaven. God gave her time to play on Earth, but it was time for her to go back. That's what I feel in my heart and I'm sticking to that." Kamren said.

"How isn't it my fault? She was supposed to be with me and she wasn't. She wasn't with me because I had some bullshit to take care of. She didn't mention the party to my parents, because she didn't want to go. In her mind, she already had plans, but I ruined that. Now she's dead and I can't get her back. I'm her brother, Kamren, and big brothers are supposed to protect their little sisters. I've always protected her, I've always made the monsters in the closet go away, and I've always kissed every booboo and made the pain go away. ONE time, Kamren, this one time, I didn't do my job!!! I will never forgive myself and neither will my family."

"I know I can't make you feel different, but I can do one thing. I can be here for you as much as possible."

"I'm ready to get my life together, but don't give up on me."

"What?"

"I said I'm ready to get my life together and I mean that. If I would have been living right, I would have been home." Brody said.

"Okay, but you have to stop blaming yourself for this. I won't give up on you, I was never giving up on you. I will be here every step of the way." Kamren said.

"Could you imagine this sweet and innocent little girl crying for someone to save her? That shit is killing me every time I think about!!"

"You need to stop thinking about it." Kamren said.

"It's kind of hard not to." Kamren rubbed Brody's hairy face and gently kissed his cheek.

"Let's move, I don't want to be here anymore. Are you down for that?"

"What do you mean move? Like into a new house or something?" Kamren asked.

"A new house, city, and state. I swear, Kamren, if I stay here, I will lose my mind."

"Are you serious about this? This is a big move and I don't want you to make a decision like this while you're grieving. You're an emotional wreck and you aren't thinking straight."

"I'm thinking straight enough to know what I want. My emotions don't even anything to do with my decision to leave. I'm going to ask you again, are you down?"

"You know I'm down until the wheels fall off. If this is going to help you heal, I'm with it. I have one question though." The sound of thunder began to rumble through the city. Brody looked at the sky and stood to his feet. He grabbed Kamren by the hand as she stood up. As they walked into the house, the rain fell. They rushed into the house and Brody closed the door. He sat on the couch in silence and stared the wall. Kamren sat next to him and kicked her boots off.

"What's your question?" He asked.

"Where are we moving?"

"We're moving to Arkansas, Little Rock, to be exact. I know that was going to be your next question." He chuckled.

"Arkansas, why there? Not Texas, Georgia, Florida, or California?" She laughed.

"Naw, I want something different, but are you cool with that?" Brody asked.

"I'm cool with whatever you're cool with. Can I tell you something?" She asked.

"What's up?"

"I'm proud of you. I hate that a change had to come because of this, but I'm still proud of you. I know it's going to take some time to heal from this. Seeing you so hurt is killing me, but I have to stay strong for the both of us."

"I'm going to miss her so much, I miss her already." He said.

"I know, baby, I miss her too. I'm not hurting like you, but I am hurting. Natasha was like my sister and the reason I wanted a baby," Kamren crossed her legs and wiped her tears. She tried her best to stay strong, but she couldn't.

"I know I put you through a lot, and I'm sorry. I had no reason to have you so worried about me."

"It's okay, I forgive you." Kamren said.

"I thank God that you never left me." He said.

"I told you from day one, B. As long as you never cheat on me, I'll never leave your side. I can't imagine life without you." Kamren smiled, and kissed the tip of Brody's flat nose.

"I wonder what good I have done to be blessed with a woman like you."

"HHhhmmm, I'm not sure, but keep doing it. I'll be around forever and a day." She laughed.

"You're so cheesy, but I love it. It's not a lot of girls like you out there. Majority of them are trying to be something they are not."

"Pretending to be someone is hard work. That's like a second job and if I'm not getting paid, I don't want a second job."

"Speaking of jobs, you need to get some rest. You have work in three hours." Brody said.

"I'm good, baby, don't worry about me. Valerie works tomorrow, and she'll pick up my slack while I take a nap here and there. Everything is going to be okay, baby. You are one of the toughest guys I know."

"I am? Because right now, I don't feel like it. It's crazy how your world can come tumbling down in seconds."

"I know, but this should be a lesson for all of us. Your life can be taken, just like that. You have to get right with the Lord before it's too late, baby."

"I am, and I will, baby, I lost Natasha, I can't lose you too." Brody said.

"Do you mean that, Brody, honestly?" She asked.

"Yea, I do, from the bottom of my heart, I do. You know what I can't wait for?" He asked.

"What is that?" Kamren asked.

"I can't wait to see you in a beautiful wedding dress. I know this might sound corny, but I dreamed about that day plenty of times."

"When will this day be?" Kamren smiled, and straddled on top of Brody's lap. He grabbed her ass cheeks and said, "it's a surprise and it's staying that way."

"Ugghhh, whatever, B, it better be worth the wait. We're not getting any younger."

"Should have married me the first time I asked you." He laughed.

"Annnnnnyyyyywwaaayyyssss, when are you telling everyone about the move?" She asked.

"I'm telling my mom and friends tomorrow, but what about you?? You know your mom is going to be all dramatic and shit."

"She might pass out and catch a heart attack. That's what happens when you are the only child." She shook her head and smacked her lips. She pictured her mom falling on the floor and passing out. She started to laugh.

"Speaking of child, have you spoken to Valerie about her in laws?" Brody laughed and rubbed his face. He was glad it wasn't being the center of attention this time.

"No, not yet, but I did call her twice. She hasn't called me back yet. I hope she isn't in jail for beating Tyson's mom." Kamren laughed.

"Fuck it, if she is, we'll bond her out." He chuckled.

"You know your ass isn't going anywhere around a police station."

"That's what I have you for. Pay the bond and we right out. That entire situation is crazy yo, I thought my family was bad off. This has nothing on us and you can admit that."

"Yes, and that is sad, because your family is fucked up."

"Thanks for mentioning it again." Brody said.

"You're welcome." She laughed.

"I feel bad for all them though, well, expect their dad. He knew better, so he should have done better! How do you ignore two children like they don't exist? I could never do that to my kids, not in a million years. No one would ever come before them."

"I guess love can make you do crazy things. I pray to God I never love like that. That kind of love is sick and twisted." Kamren yawned, but quickly closed her mouth. She grabbed the red fleece blanket and covered their bodies with it.

"I guess so, but that's toxic love." Brody pulled Kamren closer to her and kissed her floor hair. He pulled her soft hair out of the ponytail holder and massaged her scalp. Her eyes started to roll back, and she shivered.

"I can't wait to see you as a father. Are you going to trade in your classic Caprice for a van?" She asked and laughed.

"Not no, but HELL no. After that, you're going want me to wear Dockers and collar shirts with no name brand." He laughed. "OMG, I can picture you know, a straight L seven."

"I could never be a lame, baby."

"I know, baby, you're the coolest guy I know."

Within thirty minutes, Kamren fell asleep on the couch. Brody was tried, but he didn't want to sleep. He had too much on his mind for that. His cell phone started to vibrate, and it was Big Head. He rushed to silence the phone so it wouldn't wake Kamren.

Brody slowly stood to his feet and tiptoed out of the living room. He pressed the declined button, but Big Head called again. Once Brody was further down the hall, he answered the call, but in a low tone.

"Hello?"

"Nigga, why you didn't answer the first time, and why are you whispering?" Big Head's loud talking annoyed Brody. While he was trying to whisper and hide from Kamren, Big Head wasn't.

"Nigga, Kamren was sleeping on my chest, I didn't want to wake her!"

"Well, wipe the crust out of your eyes and grab your iron. We have work to do, I'm on my way to your house now."

"Naw, I can't do it, I'm done, Head, and you can let everyone know that."

"Done with what?" Big Head asked.

"You know what I'm talking about, don't make me say it over the phone."

"Are you serious right now?" The volume of Big Head's voice increased by the second. He still spoke through a closed mouth, but Brody could tell he was upset. With all that Brody was dealing with right now, Big Head had no reason to be upset or angry.

"Yea, I'm very serious, I can't do this shit anymore. It's fucking up my life right before my eyes. My little sister was supposed to be with me, and not at that party. I lost my sister, and if I keep it up, I'm going to lose my girl."

"You're going to let a death, and some pussy, stop you from getting this money? I thought you had more sense than that." Big Head shook his head and chuckled.

"My nigga, you need to watch your mouth!! You're talking reckless right now. That death was my fucking sister, and that piece of pussy is my girl. The same girl I've been with, this ain't a piece of random pussy."

"She finally got to you." Big Head chuckling pissed Brody off. He wanted to disconnect the call, but wanted to hear what he had to say.

"What do you mean, 'got to me?' She didn't get to me, my common sense did. I wish yours would get to you to, but I don't see that happening."

"B, I understand all that, I really do, but this is big bucks I'm talking. No whammies, $4,000 a head. It's four guys. This can be your last hit, think about it. Why not go out with a bang and show them clowns how you really get down?" Brody was quiet, he was in deep thought. He looked at his closet and pictured his dessert eagle that was on the floor. Then he looked at his tennis shoes that were placed in front of the closet.

"Last one, huh?" He asked.

"Yea, last one." Brody was still thinking, but his mind was in another place. He made a lot of promises to Kamren, but was he strong enough to keep them? The streets were like a drug, but no one wanted to admit it. After one fast night of selling drugs or jacking, you were hooked on that high. Every day, you chased that same high, but you could never find it again. That's how the streets got you, it pretends to love you, but it doesn't. It doesn't love anyone, but even itself. It strips you from your family and friends and turn you into another person. A person that your love ones can no longer recognize or tolerate to be in their presence.

"I'm two minutes away from your house, are you ready?" Brody removed the phone from his ear and exhaled.

Kamren stood in the hall way with her hands on her hips. Brody knew he was caught so he disconnected the call without telling Big Head.

"I guess you were talking just to hear yourself. Damn, Brody, for a moment, I believed you. I believed everything you said, like a fucking fool."

"Kamren, you have it all wrong." Brody said.

"No, I don't, you were going to sneak off with Big Head. What is it, a robbery or a hit? Which one are you risking your life for? You know one wrong move, and you'll be lying next to your sister!!"

"KAMREN, SHUT UP AND LISTEN!!! I'M NOT GOING ANYWHERE, AND THAT'S WHAT I TOLD HIM. As of today, I'm done with it, I'm done for good and nothing can change my mind."

"Do you mean that, Brody?"

"Yes, now give me a kiss."

"No, but you can kiss my ass." She shouted.

"Hhhmm, you know I would love to do that," Brody smirked and licked his lips. The way he sized Kamren up and down, she knew what was on his mind. She tried to play serious, but she couldn't. Kamren burst into laughter and unbuckled her shorts. She dropped them to the floor and pulled her shirt over her head. Brody walked to Kamren and scooped her into his arms. He couldn't wait until they got upstairs to get it on. He nibbled on her bare breasts and kissed her neck. Her naked body felt amazing in his hands. Tonight, he was going to make sure Kamren reached an ecstasy she didn't know existed.

Chapter 6

Brody and Savage sat on Savage's porch, sipping codeine, with a fat blunt full of kush in rotation. He was serious about his change, but these habits were going to take some time to fade away. His stress level was high, and his patience was low. He couldn't get his mind off his sister, and at any given moment, he wanted to spazz out. If anyone looked at him wrong, he wanted to start a fight.

"I have to tell you something, my nigga." Brody said.

"What's up, fool?" He asked.

"I decided last night that Kamren and I are moving."

"Moving, moving where, into a new house?" Savage asked.

"Yea, but in a new state." Brody said.

"What?"

"We're moving to Arkansas, it's time for me to get my head together. All this with my little sister has messed with my head." "Are you serious?" Savage asked. He was hoping Brody wasn't serious.

"Yea, in that time, I can focus on getting myself together, so I can run for mayor."

"You're serious about this?"

"Yea and my mind is made up. Kamren is down for it also. Besides our parents, you're the only person I told. Well, I'm pretty sure Kam told Valerie, but that's it. I'm done with all this street shit, but Big Head isn't feeling it. We kind of got into an argument last night, but fuck him."

"So that's why he wanted me to handle that with him." Savage said.

"Basically, but I'm serious, Savage, I'm done with robbing and being a shooter."

"I feel you, man, do what's best for you. Big Head is content living like this. That nigga doesn't have any understanding. All he knows is guns and stick ups. It's way more to life than that. If we continue to live like this, we won't see what life can bring us." Savage said.

"Thanks for having my back, man," Brody dapped Savage down and took a gulp of his drink.

"You know that, big brother. Besides, Arkansas isn't far, I can visit anytime. I've been thinking about something lately. It's been on my mind heavily and I don't know what to do." Savage said.

"Thinking about what?" Brody asked. He slowly sipped the codeine and took a hit of the blunt. The ice cold and sweet drank was good, but it wasn't enough for him. It wasn't helping him grieve, it only made him sleepy.

"This relationship thing isn't for me. My girl and I aren't how we used to be. I think we're growing apart, that's crazy. You're Dr. Love, you tell me what's going on." Savage said.

"What's going on with y'all? I thought everything was going good."

"I thought so too, but I guess not. I feel like it's a distance between us and I can't fix it. Sometimes, when I touch her, she pulls away and we haven't had sex in a week." Savage said.
"Maybe her period is on, you know how they can be during that time of the month." Brody said.

"No, it isn't that, I checked while she was sleeping." He laughed.

"Damn, my brother, it sounds like she's cheating on you," Brody grabbed the blunt out of Savage's hand and took. By the way Savage was looking, he could tell everything was making sense in his head.

"She has come home late days this week. She always has her phone in her hand and now she has a passcode on it. Rachel never had a passcode on her phone before. I think.... I'm getting played, that bitch."

"I hate to say it again, but she is cheating on you." Brody said.

"No, she can't be cheating on me. I'm too good for her to do something like that."

"I don't know, Savage, but you need to talk to her. I'd rather you know sooner, than later. If she isn't cheating on you, you she needs to tell you what's wrong."

"I know, I'll try and talk to her when she comes home tonight." Savage said.

"Where is she anyways?" Brody asked.

"Now that you mentioned it, I don't know. She was off from work today, so she isn't there. This morning she told me she was going to her mom's house. I guess she's still there, shit, I don't know."

Savage pulled his phone out of his pocket and slid his thumb across the screen. Once his phone was unlocked he scrolled to the Facebook application. He wasn't the time to lurk through his girlfriend's social media accounts, but today, he was that guy.

He logged into her Facebook account and he was surprised that the password was still his name and birthday.

"Are you on her Facebook?" Brody asked.

"Yea," Savage scrolled through the messages and one particular message caught his attention. She told a guy named Deshawn, that she couldn't wait to see him tonight. Savage clicked the messages and began to read them. Rachel was talking to this guy for little over a month. By the sexual things she told him, she had a serious thing for him.

Reading the messages made him furious, but he had to calm himself down. He inhaled and exhaled, then he clicked onto the guy's Facebook profile. He didn't recognize the guy, at all, but he was from Opelousas. Savage handed Brody his phone and said, "do you know him?" Brody placed his cup next to him and held the phone closer to his eyes.

"Yea, that's Deshawn from Linwood."

"Who?" Savage asked.

"That's Deshawn Peterson from Linwood. He was locked in Hunts for about two years. I think he was there for a dope charge, but he got out four months ago. I didn't know you fucked with him."

"I don't know this clown, but I think Rachel is messing with him."

"What, how did you come to that conclusion already?" Brody laughed.

"Because she's been talking to him on Facebook." Savage fumbled back to the messages and Brody began to read them. His facial expressions said it all and he stopped reading the messages. He could no longer read the sexual and freaky things Rachel said to Deshawn. Deshawn was a clown ass nigga, but thought jail made him a real nigga. He only went to jail for a dope charge, because his brother made him take the charge. Rumors circulated town that Deshawn was someone's bitch in jail. He never denied the rumors, and that gave everyone their answer.

"Rachel does that with her mouth? I've been with Kam for how long? And I can't get her to do that." Brody laughed.

"She doesn't do it to me. I didn't know she could open her mouth that wide." Savage said.

"Damn, I guess you learn something new every day."

"This explains why she changed her password and always has her phone. She's meeting up with him today, but I wonder if she's there now. Should I go with my move or go with my move?"

"Either way, you're going with your move. I'm diving behind you, head first. You want to go to Linwood?" Brody asked.

"Hell yea, let's go." Brody and Savage stood to their feet. Savage quickly ran to his door and locked it. Brody grabbed his gun that was under the steps and walked to Savage's car. They both got in and drove off.

Savage increased the volume on his radio and let the UGK music blast through his speakers. The music was too loud for Brody to talk. He would see how angry Savage was, but he couldn't blame him. The things Rachel said in the messages surprised Brody. He always thought she was the quiet type, but now he knew she wasn't.

He turned into the quiet neighborhood and crept through the streets. Brody pointed to the tan house that was located at the corner. Rachel's car was parked at the house and Savage was ready to flip out.

"Oh boy." Brody shook his head and mumbled.

"Yea, you got that right, I should kill this stupid bitch, B."

Savage pulled into the driveway at the unknown house. Brody already knew what Savage was going to do, and he wasn't going to stop him. Rachael was a no-good bitch for cheating on Savage. From day one, he gave her the world and more. Anything she wanted to do, he had her back. Savage knew he could be jumping to a conclusion, but he couldn't help it. All the evidence was in his face and he couldn't help the way he was feeling.

"I should break the bitch's window for being here. Then her dumb ass will have to ride home in the cold."

"Fuck it," Brody pulled the gun from his waist and rammed the handle of the gun into the window. Brody laughed as the glass shattered everywhere. Brody tucked the gun back on his waist and they walked to the door. He could care less about damaging Rachel's window. He needed someone, or something, to take his frustration out on.

Savage knocked on the door and waited for someone to answer. He could hear someone walking to the door and clear their throat. He noticed a peephole on the door and he cover it with his thumb.

"What are we going to do?" Brody asked.

"I don't know, whatever the fuck we want to do." Savage said, making Brody laugh.

"Who is it?" The guy shouted, but he didn't open the door. Savage looked at Brody then said, "it's me, nigga."

"It's me, man, now open the door, it's cold as a mug out here."

"Oh, okay." Brody shook his hand and snickered. He couldn't believe the guy was answering the door. That wasn't something Brody, True Love, Big Head, or Savage, would have done.

The guy opened the door, but he looked confused. He sat his cigarette on the stool and said, "nigga, you ain't Jack, who are you?"

"It doesn't matter who I am. Where is Deshawn? I need to ask him something." Savage said.

"First, you need to say who you are. You won't walk in this bitch like you own the place." The slim guy leaned back and crossed his arms his small chest. Savage and Brody looked at one another and burst into laughter.

"B, he said we won't walk in this bitch like we own the place."

"I heard him, loud and clear. You want to show him how we walk into any place like we own the building?" Brody asked.

"Yea, I think we should show him how it's done," Savage cocked his tight fist back, then he rammed it into the guys face. He fell straight backwards and landed on his back. Brody and Savage laughed as they walked over his body. Brody looked back again and laughter harder.

Savage walked down the hall opening the door to the rooms, but Rachel was nowhere in sight. He turned around, but the sound of giggling stopped him. He nodded his head towards Brody and he followed behind him. Savage took a few steps back and kicked the door. The raggedy door came off the hinges falling to the floor. Rachel screamed, but her eyes stretched wide when she noticed it was Brody and Savage. Savage wasn't surprised that he caught her, but Brody was shocked that he was right. Rachel was caught in act, butt ass naked and couldn't lie her way out of this.

"Oh my God, Brandon, what are you doing here?" Rachel grabbed the pillow to cover her body. She was clueless to why Savage had Brody with him. The last thing she wanted was Brody to forever have an image of her naked body in his head.

"What are you doing here? I thought you were at your mom's, bitch, you lied!"

"Rachel, who are these two clowns?" Deshawn didn't care that he was naked. He jumped to his feet, using both hands to point at Savage and Brody.

"I'm her boyfriend, but I'm not here for you, fall back, homie. I'm here for her, Rachel what the fuck are you doing here?"

"I- I- I- I can explain, Brandon, give me a minute," Rachel stared at the floor, looking for her panties, but she couldn't find them. Brody tried to not stare at her, but he couldn't avoid the ass and breasts that were a few feet away from him. This was uncomfortable for him, he was sure his presence made Rachel feel the same way.

"How are you going to explain it, Rachel? I would love to hear this shit. Brody, wouldn't you love to hear her explain why she's here?"

"Yea, I would, I have time to listen." He chuckled dropping his head. In a discreet way, Deshawn tried to grab his wooden bat, but he wasn't fast enough. Pointing the gun at Deshawn, Brody said, "put the bat down, playboy." Looking dead in the barrel with his heart pounding out his chest, Deshawn didn't drop the bat. In Brody's eyes, his actions were pussy, Brody witness plenty of pussy niggas play the tough role minutes before begging for their lives.

"Oh, you're a tuff guy now? Well let's see how tuff you are." Taking his gun off safety, Brody then pointed it directly at Deshawn's head. Rachel cried louder begging. "Please, Brody, don't shoot him!"

Deshawn slowly dropped the bat on the floor, dropping to his knees. Brody could see Deshawn shaking with his knees buckling like a belt.

"You're not so tuff now, huh? Sit down before these bullets make you do backflips." Brody said.

"Matter of fact, I want everything you have. Guns, drugs, money, whatever you got!"

"Man, I don't have nothing!"

"Nigga, stop lying, do what he said before it gets ugly in here. This is my last time talking to you," Brody raised his foot in the air kicking Deshawn in his rib cage. Rachel shouted again, but this time, she sobbed, instead of crying. Deshawn rolled on the ground in the fetal position in pain. It felt like his ribs were on fire, Deshawn needed a doctor as soon as possible. In this moment, he regretted replying to Rachel's message. He didn't think a pretty girl like her could bring this kind of drama to his life.

"STOP IT, JUST STOP IT, WHY ARE Y'ALL DOING THIS?"

"SHUT THE FUCK UP, RACHEL, EVERYTHING YOU'RE DOING RIGHT NOW IS ANNOYING ME." Savage shouted, rubbing his temples. Everything about Rachel annoyed him and he wanted to make that clear to her.

Brody grabbed Deshawn by his long neck, tossing him to Savage with a grin on his face. When Brody heard footsteps, he quickly turned around with his finger clutching the trigger. It was the guy he knocked out, stumbling into the room, looking for more trouble. Brody smacked his lips saying, "oh, look who finally decided to wake up."

"What's going on?" The guy's head was spinning, he could hardly keep his eyes open. He rubbed his temples to stop the pain, but it didn't work. Brody punched him again, making him fall to the floor. Rachel opened her mouth to scream again, but Savage gave her a dirty look. She covered her face with the pillow silently crying, she wasn't a fool to make a noise.

Brody tapped on the guys pocket feeling a large knot in his right pocket. Shuffling in it, staring at the guy, he pulled out a stack of money. Brody laughed, tossing it to Savage. With quick hands, Savage caught the money stuffing it into his pocket.

"Where the fuck is the rest of the money? If you don't tell me, I'm going to blow your brains out. Give me your gun," Savage told Deshawn. Brody walked to Savage, handing him another gun that was attached to his hip. He placed his finger on the trigger, making Deshawn's eyes grow big. He pointed at the closet tossing his hands in the air. Savage grabbed him by the neck to drag him to the closet and open the door. Spotting the bag plastic bag full of money made Savage grinned like the Joker. He wasn't in need of the money, he was far from hurtin', but he liked taking what wasn't his.

Still holding Deshawn by the neck, who could hardly breathe, Savage scanned the closet finding a roll of black duct tape. Before grabbing it, he tossed the plastic bag to Brody who had his eyes glued to Rachel. If she made any wrong move, Brody was going to have to hit her where it hurts.

Savage pulled a few long pieces of the tape covering Deshawn's mouth with his. Then he placed Deshawn's wrists together wrapping them with the tape tightly. He wanted Deshawn to temporarily lose the feeling in his hands just in case he would try and do anything. Once he was done, he kicked Deshawn in the chest, making him fall backwards into the closet.

"Brandon, you and Brody need to leave. Your name is already ringing in the streets. You don't need any more trouble following your name. "

"That's the last thing you should be worried about. You're fucking some nigga in a trap house. How desperate can you get, you're looking for love that damn bad? I thought you were better than this, Rachel, but you're just like the rest of them hoes. Don't bother coming to my house to come get any of your shit. I'll burn it before I give it to you or maybe I should give it to another broad when I move her in. I'm sure she's going to love those designer bags I brought you."

"WHAT?" Rachel stood to her feet, running across the dirty, sheet less bed. Rachel was so shocked by Savage's words, that she forgot she was naked running behind him. He ignored her, walking out of the door, he was done with her dumb ass, but she wasn't done with him. Rachel grabbed a hoodie from the floor quickly putting it on. Since it was a size 2x, it covered majority of her body.

"Brandon, wait, let me talk!"

"Talk about what? Girl, we don't have nothing to talk about. I'm done with your ass and I'm on to the next one. Someone is going to appreciate me, I'm a good ass nigga."

"You're never home, some days I don't see you at all. What did you expect me to do, Brandon, huh? Tell me! I'm supposed to be alone while you're in the streets doing God knows what!?!!!"

"You know what the fuck I was doing!! You said you were okay with it. Maybe you were okay with it because you were fucking another guy. You and I both know every time you called me to come home, I did!! I did every single thing you asked me, Rachel, and I have to find out you're cheating on me like this. If you didn't want to be with me anymore, you should have told me that. Shit didn't have to end like this, but it's all good though. I wish you the best with whoever you deal with from this point on."

"I wanted to tell you, but I wasn't sure how to. I didn't want to leave you, but I needed attention. You weren't giving me any attention, Brandon. Brody sees you more than I do. Shit, Kamren sees you more than I do."

"Hey, keep my girl's name out of your mouth. She doesn't have anything to do with this." Brody snapped.

"You didn't cheat because of me. You cheated because you're a stupid hoe, that's what you wanted to do!"

"A hoe, excuse me?"

"You heard what the fuck I said, you can quit with the innocent act. I just witnessed a nigga bend you over in a way I never have. If you needed attention, that's all you had to say. I would have given you my own life to show you how much you meant to me."

"Sometimes, you acted like you didn't love me. That's a hurtful feeling, you know that." Rachel said.

"Quit with the bullshit, Rachel!! If I didn't love you, I would knock your teeth out of your mouth. Now get away from my car or you'll be dragged with it." Savage pushed Rachel out of his way and got into his car. She lost her balance and stumbled to the ground. The grass was wet, cold, and felt uncomfortable against her body. Rachel sat on her knees crying, but that didn't stop Savage from driving off. He was done with Rachel and he meant that.

"Are you good, Savage?" Brody asked.

"Yea, I'm good, thanks for having my back in there."

"You know you don't have to thank me, that's on the muscle."

Chapter 7

It was noon, but Brody was still in bed sleeping. His head was banging, it felt like he had a migraine approaching. He slowly opened his eyes and found Kamren standing next to the bed. Her chest was expanding up and down and her foot was tapping against the floor. Her lips her tight, but her eyes were tighter staring at him. Brody could barely see the white area of her eyes. He rubbed his face and said, "good morning, baby, what's up with you?"

"I'm going to ask you this one time, and you better tell me the truth. If you don't, I swear, I'm packing my shit and leaving."

"What the hell is wrong with you, Kamren?" He said.

"Where were you last night, Brody?"

"I was with Savage and you know that."

"Where else did you to go?" She asked. Brody could tell Kamren knew something, so it was no reason to play stupid. He pushed the comforter set off his body and rolled out of bed.

Kamren raced down the stairs and Brody ran behind her. She grabbed her purse, but he stopped her. She turned around and mugged him. He released her hand and took three steps backward.

"Kamren, I can explain."

"What do you have to explain, Brody? Are you going to explain how you lied to me?" Kamren asked. "Technically, I didn't lie, none of that was my fault. I got pulled into some mess with Savage and I reacted. If you calm down and stay I will explain everything." Kamren thought about it for a few seconds. She could barely tolerate looking at Brody, but she wanted to hear what he had to say.

She placed her purse and the corner top and sat down. She pulled Brody's chair out and pointed at the chair.

"Have a seat." She said, in a firm voice. Brody sat down and began to talk. "Like I said before, none of it was my fault, and it damn sure wasn't planned. Savage and I was sitting outside his house, doing what we do. Sipping drank and smoking weed, a boring night until you got home. He started talking about his relationship and how Rachel was acting with him lately."

"What do you mean?" Kamren asked.

"He said she started acting weird with him. She didn't want to have sex with him, or he couldn't even touch her. Rachel started coming home late, and for the first time, she put a password on her phone. He asked me, and I told him the truth. I guess the light bulb went off in his head and everything made sense. He logged into her Facebook and saw the she was talking to some guy." Brody said.

"What guy? I want to know everything."

"His name is Deshawn and he lives in Linwood." Brody said.

"Are you talking about that guy who just got out of prison?" She asked.

"Yea, but how do you know him?"

"Calm down, Brody, I don't know him. One day, Val and I were at the gas station, and he tried to get her number. You know she turned him down, but he didn't want to take no for an answer. He followed us to Raising Cane and Valerie pulled out her pepper spray. He ran like she had a gun or something." She laughed.

"What, why didn't you tell me this? I would have checked him on sight."

"See, that's why I didn't tell you. Besides, it wasn't a big deal to us. We were laughing the entire time."

"Next time something like that happens, you better tell me. I never want you to feel uncomfortable when I'm not around. Did you have your gun with you?" He asked.

"I did have it on me, but I didn't think it was that serious to pull it out."

"I guess you're right, but when we got there, Rachel's car was there." Brody said.

"What, are you for real?" Kamren asked.

"I'm for real, and when we walked into the room, she was in there with him. Rachel was ass naked, spreading her ass cheeks open, while he was beating her pussy up from the back. That girl was throwing her ass back, and had her finger in her ass, like a pornstar." He laughed.

"Don't push it, Brody, watch your mouth. I don't want to hear about what another woman was doing," Kamren pushed Brody's head and rolled her eyes. That quick, he pissed her off again.

"I'm sorry, baby, but you said you wanted to know everything. I can't lie, we did some dumb and unnecessary shit. I was acting out of anger and looking for a way to let my anger out. I'm sorry, Kamren, I wish none of last night would have happened."

For a moment, Kamren was quiet, she wasn't sure what to do say. Instead of talking, she stared out of the kitchen's sliding doors. All of a sudden, she dropped her head and laid her upper body on the table. Brody wasn't sure if she believed him or if she was mad at him.

"Brody, Brody, Brody, why do you always put me in these situations? I love you to the moon and back, but damn. What if my parents or family hear about this? What am I supposed to tell them, another lie? How many lies can I tell them? One day they will call me out on my lying and nine out of ten, you won't be around. As usual, I will be the one to defend you. I defend you, I defend myself, this relationship, and all the bad things you do. Enough is enough, Brody, you don't have any more chances. I understand you're going through something, I really do. Like I told you before, I'm hurting, but I can't feel your pain. If you are feeling yourself getting angry, please, come and talk to me. That's what I'm here for, I'm not just here to look pretty on your arm."

"I will, baby, and I'm sorry."

"I guess I can accept your apology this time. Any apologizes after this, you can keep them to yourself. Apologizing to me will be a waste of time, you got that?"

"I understand what you're saying, but are you still leaving?" Brody grabbed Kamren's hands and looked her in the eyes.

"I'm only leaving to go to the store with my mom. There is a sale at J.C. Penny and I can't miss it." She said.

"Okay, that's cool, I'm going to cook while you're gone. Any special requests for my favorite girl?"

"UUhhhhhh, no, how about you surprise me. Let's see how much you know me." She smirked.

"I know you like the back of my hand, you'll see."

"Do you think those guys will come back for war?" Kamren asked, but Brody laughed.

"I highly doubt it, Deshawn is pussy. I don't know who the other guy was. If he's friends with Deshawn, then he's pussy too." Brody said.

"Was that true about him being gay in jail?" Kamren asked.

"I don't know, I wasn't in the cell with him. If you're gay in jail, you're all around gay. It's no gray areas when it comes to that."

"Okay, enough about this gay stuff. I don't want to think about a man digging his dick in another grown man's butt hole, ugh." Kamren shook her head, causing Brody to laugh.

"How could she cheat on Savage for someone like that guy? Following us to Raising Cane was beyond thirsty."

"I guess she wanted someone thirsty. Like she said, Savage didn't show her attention. I think she was making up things, so she could cheat." Brody said.

"What? Now I even know she's lying." Kamren said.

"Right, and I'm glad we don't have those kind of problems. That cheating shit is played out."

"Our problems are deeper than cheating."

***

It's been five days since Tyson had spoken to or seen his father. He didn't have much to say to him. He didn't try to reach or explain anything to Tyson. That proved a lot to him, his dad wasn't the man he thought he was. His mom did mention to him that she told him about Joe' Ann. Dennis hardly responded, after all these years he still didn't care about her. Elise blamed herself for his lack of compassion, but it wasn't only her fault. Dennis played a role in this mess also. The fact that he allowed a woman to dictate a relationship with his child will be something he never understand.

"Did you make it there?" Valerie walked through the kitchen with a towel wrapped around her body. Her hair was dripping wet and wet footprints followed behind her. She was fresh off work and the first thing she did was run to the shower. Working in a hospital meant germs lingered on her work scrubs. She never wanted to bring home germs and pass them to Tyson. If he got sick, that meant she would have to take care of him. When Tyson was sick, he was dramatic and extra. Valerie wasn't in any mood to hear him whining and crying about his runny nose or a rough cough.

"I'm turning on the street now, I wish Elizabeth could have come." Tyson said.

"Yea, that would have been nice. The three of you could have met and talked about everything. I just hope she doesn't freak or when you tell her who you are."

"I know, that's what I'm afraid of. If she does freak out, I can't blame her. If someone tells me there my sibling at this age, I probably wouldn't embrace them with open arms." Tyson laughed.

"You and me both, I would freak out. Especially if this random person came to my home unannounced."

"Hey, you said this was a good idea. It's better than going in her Facebook messages. Then she would have thought I was and creep and blocked me." Tyson said.

"Baby, it is a good idea. If you would tell someone something like this on a social network, they're bound to ignore you. Look at you, for example. You bypassed Elizabeth's message and never looked back." Valerie grabbed the long metal spoon and scoop a large amount of spaghetti into the bowl. A little of the cold sauce got on her finger, so she licked it. Even cold, her food still tasted great.

"Rrriiigggghhhhhhttt, my point exactly, I didn't want to be labeled as a creep on social media." Tyson slowly drove down the street searching for the brick house with the red trimming. From a distance, he stopped, there was a girl casually dragging her trash to the end of the driveway. The color of the house fit the description on the house in the Facebook picture.

"I think I think I found her, let me call you back." Tyson said.

"Okay, T, good luck and I love you."

"I love you too, baby, see you at home." Tyson disconnected the call and dropped his cell on his sit. He parked his car a few feet before the house and got out of his car. Joe' Ann and Tyson locked eyes, but no one said anything. Something was telling Tyson that Joe' Ann already knew who he was.

"Uuuummmm, are you Joe' Ann?" He asked.

"Yea, I am, you're Tyson, right?"

"Yea, I take it that you already know who I am." Tyson said.

"I do, but are Alfred and Matthew coming? I'm pretty sure they want to know a few things." Joe' Ann said.

"Naw, they aren't coming. The only person that knows I'm here is my mom."

"That doesn't surprise me, let's go inside to talk."

"Okay, cool." Joe' Ann motioned for Tyson to followed her and he did. They walked into the cold house and she closed the door behind him. The house smelled of lime and lemons. A mop bucket was in the middle of the floor, so he figured Joe' Ann was in the middle of cleaning.

"You can have a seat on the couch," Joe' Ann walked to the couch and grabbed her MacBook. Tyson sat down and she across from him. He discretely looked around the living room to observe things. The house was nice, but he wondered if it was her home.

"Nice place you have here."

"Thank you, my husband and I purchased it about a year ago." She said.

"Oh okay, is your husband here?" He asked.

"No, but he'll be back home tomorrow. He works offshore, but my son is in the room sleeping."

"Family woman, I see, I like that." He chuckled.

"Yea, I try to be, but do you have kids?" She asked.

"No, not yet, my girlfriend and I are trying to have one." Tyson said.

"Aaawww, congratulations, I hope it works out for you two." She smiled, fully exposing her blue braces.

"Thank you, I appreciate that. So, have you spoken to my mother?" He asked.

"Yea, I did, and she told me everything that happened. It seems like Dad is worse than I think. On top of not be able to talk my brothers, I find out I have a sister. Can Ashton Kutcher come out with the cameras? Dad had to call the show, so they could punk us," Joan crossed her legs and laughed. Tyson shook his head and laughed as hell.

"That's the same thing I told my girlfriend. I never heard of some shit like this happening before. Can you believe he had three women pregnant, but made MY mom, his wife, have an abortion?"

"No, I can't believe none of it! You have to be a sick person to do any of this. Your mom didn't tell me much about our sister. Her name is Elizabeth, right?" Joe' Ann asked.

"Yea, it's Elizabeth, and her and I are the same age. We're six months apart actually, but she looks mature for her age. She's a psychologist and has her own business in Lawtell. Elizabeth is a nice girl, but I definitely see Dad's bad side in her." Tyson said.

"Wow, I don't think that's a good thing, and especially for a woman. How did you find out she's our sister?" Joe 'Ann asked.

"To make a long story short, she reached out to me. Her mom had her thinking someone else was her dad. She finally told her the truth and she went from there."

"Wow, how awkward was that?" She laughed.

"Hella awkward, but I'm glad she reached out. We all have the right to know one another and have the option to be in each other's lives. I know this is crazy, and I don't expect you to jump into the family like everything is gravy."

"It is crazy, but let's get something straight. I don't hate you, now your mom and dad, that's a different story. I can't see me being a family with Dad, but I can see us forming a relationship. The things my mom told me about dad, I pray I NEVER fall in love with a man like that. We couldn't go to the same school you guys did, because my mom was afraid of what my dad and your mom would do to me. It's been numerous times I've seen Dad, and he wouldn't look my way. Sometimes, it hurt me, but after a while, I didn't look his way either."

"How did you and my mom start communicating?" Tyson asked.

"I guess after a while, she couldn't take it anymore. She reached out to me, but behind Dad's back. She basically tried to make up with showering me with love. I pretended that it worked, but it didn't. She was the reason Dad wasn't in my life. I could never forgive her for that. Not having a father in my life was hard, and for days, the thought of it made me cry."

"I understand that, but it's not just her fault. He could have put his foot down and handled his business like a man. No woman could ever come before my child or children. I don't care how sexy or pretty she is."

"Right, and a woman should never make a man choose between her and his kids." Joe'Ann said.

"My mom said she hadn't spoken to you in a year. Did something happen, or did you two lose contact?" Tyson asked.

"I stopped talking to her actually. Your dad found out she was talking to me and he flipped out. He told her she better stop talking to me or things would get ugly for the both of us. Then, two months later, she tried to reach out to me. Of course, she had a fat check of $3,000 to buy my love back, but I declined it. I changed my number and never looked back," Joe'Ann shrugged her shoulders, but a sad look was also on her face. Tyson could tell reliving her past made her emotional.

"Damn, that's hard, and I hate you had to go through that. Those are the kind of things that scars a person for life." He said.

"It did at one point in time, but I'm okay now. I have my own little family that I love, and they love me back. Dad can continue to act like I don't exist, and I will do the same about him. I think it's the best for everyone."

"I understand that, I know I can't make you change your mind. If I were you, I would probably feel the same way as well. As long as us as siblings come together, I'm okay with that. I spoke to Elizabeth earlier, and she can't wait to meet you."

"Are you serious?" She smiled and asked.

"Yea." Tyson said.

"That's a bet, we all should link up soon. What about Matthew and Alfred? What do they have to say about this? Do they even want to meet me?" She asked.

"Honestly, I haven't talked to them about it yet. They're still trying to get over what happened."

"Okay, I guess we have to wait and see what they have to say." She said.
"My girlfriend's best friend and boyfriend are moving soon. They're going to have a dinner at his parent's house. You and Elizabeth are more than welcome to come with me."

"Are you sure about that? That seems like a family affair and I don't want to intrude." She said.

"Not at all, they'll welcome you with open arms." Tyson said.

"I remember when I saw you in the club, about three years ago. I think we were at Club Karma the night of Christmas. I'm not sure if it was the Patron, but I had the urge to introduction myself to you. I wanted to tell you everything right then and there, but my friend said no. It wasn't the time or place to discuss any of that. She was right, but I still regret not talking to you. Besides seeing you on the pass by, I don't see you much." She said.

"That's because I work a lot and we don't live in town." Tyson said.

"That makes sense, I'm guessing the girl I see you with is your girlfriend."

"Yea, her name is Valerie, and she's an E.R. nurse." Tyson was a little nervous, his hands were beginning to sweat. He wiped them on his shirt and tucked them into his pockets.

He tried not to stare at Joe' Ann too much, but he couldn't help it. Just like Elizabeth, she looked a lot like their father.

"Hhhmm, a nurse, that's fancy." She laughed.

Tyson and Joe' Ann talked for hours. It felt like they knew one another all their lives.

After talking to Elizabeth and explaining to her how nice Joe' Ann was, she was dying to meet her. She decided to leave work and take a trip to her house.

Joe' Ann was nervous, she wasn't sure how her and Elizabeth would vibe with one another. They could be the total opposite, and not get along, or they could the same and get along well.

"I hope she likes me, this is a weird situation, Tyson," Joe' Ann stood in the living room mirror, brushing her hair. She knew how females judged hair and she wanted to make sure her hair was perfect.

"You're worrying for no reason, she's going to love you, Joe." Tyson said.

"You want to know something, when I was little, I hated the nickname Joe. I always felt like people were calling me a boy, but now I love it. People call me Joe all day long. Some people call me Joe Joe." She laughed.

"Joe Joe, like the singer?" He asked and laughed.

"Yep, just like the singer." She laughed.

"What if you would have dated Elizabeth or me? Dad would have passed out when you would have brought us home." She chuckled and shook her head.

"Man, that would have been a sight to see. When he's nervous, he instantly turnes pale." He laughed.

Joe' Ann stared out of her window and spotted a red Infiniti truck pulling into her driveway. She dropped her brush and squealed. Tyson closed his eyes and covered his ears. Joe' Ann grabbed his arm and pulled him to his feet. They walked to the door and waited for Elizabeth to approach the door. Joe' Ann couldn't wait, she opened the door and waved at Elizabeth. Elizabeth smiled back and said, "hi, you must be Joe' Ann."

"I am and it's nice to meet you," she said.

"It's nice to me you as well, sis," Elizabeth started to cry, but she wiped her tears. She gave Joe'Ann a big hug and cried harder. Joe' Ann fanned her eyes to make the water evaporate, but it didn't. She couldn't fight back her tears anymore. This was a special moment for her and she had no reason to hide her emotions. Tyson also started to cry and hug his sister. Finally, their family was complete.

***

Brody sat in small church room, with tears dripping down his smooth face. Being a part of the funeral was too much handle. The sight of his baby sister in a pink casket, didn't sit well with him. Her pink dress and big white hair bows made her look like a limited-edition Barbie doll.

All her friends were escorted to the funeral by their parents or guardian. Some cried, but others didn't. They seemed confused to what was going on.

Seeing all the love their daughter was getting, made Brody Senior and Patty's hearts warm. The feeling was great, but it didn't fully mend the pain they were feeling.

"Where the hell are my cigarettes?" Brody looked to his left and right, but his box of Kools were nowhere in sight.

He patted on his pockets, but the only things he felt were his keys and a roll of money.

"Damn, man." He whispered and grabbed his head. He was stressing bad and needed that nicotine to calm his nerves.

"Are you looking for these?" Kamren stood in the door frame with her arm extended to Brody. She was dress in all black with a big church head. Her head was tilted over a face a little, but Brody could hardly get a good look at her.

He nodded his head and grabbed the cigarettes out of Kamren's hand and said, "thanks, baby, but where did you find my cigarettes?" Brody patted his pockets for his lighter, but he stopped. For a second, he thought about lighting his cigarette in the church. He knew Kamren would catch a fit or probably even hit him.

"They fell out of your pockets when you were walking away from the casket. I could tell you wanted to be alone, that's why I didn't follow behind you."

"It's all good, baby, I just needed some time to clear my head. It's still kind of hard to see her in a casket." Brody said.

"I know, baby, but she's beautiful and looks peaceful. Look at how many people came to show their respect to her. She was loved by so many people, she's going to be truly missed."

"I wish I could go to the movies with her one more time, baby. That's all I need to get better, but I know it won't happen."

"We just have to find other ways to make it better, Brody. Now you have your two-favorite people watching over you, it must be nice," Kamren removed her hat from her head and sat next to Brody. She fluffed her fluffy hair a little and exhaled. She wasn't sure what she could say that would make Brody feel better. All she could do is be the shoulder he cried and that he did a lot.

"I know right, I bet she ran to my grandfather when she got to Heaven," Brody cried and laughed at the same time. His hands were wet because of the fallen tears. He wiped his hands against his silk shirt and reached for the roll of toilet tissue. He stared at the cheap toilet tissue and laughed. The tissue was the almost the same color of clay and looked rough. The church made plenty of money, but didn't provide their members with decent tissue.

He knew Natasha and his grandfather were having a blast in Heaven. He couldn't get their smiles out of his head, but he didn't want to. Those warm smiles mended his pain a little.

"I swear, Brody, if I could take your pain away, I would. I would give everything I have just to see you smile again." Kamren said, but she stopped talking. She felt like she didn't have Brody's undivided attention while they were talking. She reached to rub his leg, but he grabbed her hand and gave it a kiss.

"I know you would, baby, that's why I love you. I'll get my smile back, but not today." Brody said.
"I understand that, like I told you before, take your time. Don't rush the healing process to please others."

"I won't, baby, and I love you," Brody wrapped his arm around Kamren's neck, and gave her a hug. She kissed his lips and grabbed his hair. She stood to her feet and pulled him to his feet as well. Brody's body seemed slimmer than it was a week ago. Not only was he stressing, he was also started to lose weight.

"I love you more, now let's go. I know your mom and everyone else is looking for us."

"Yea, you're right."

Kamren and Brody walked out of the room, but noticed a familiar face standing in the breezeway. It was Big Head, and for some reason, he looked like he was up to no good. The smell of cigarettes was heavy on his black hoodie and jeans.

"What's he doing here?" Kamren whispered to Brody.

"I don't know, but I'm going to find out." Since the argument between Brody and Big Head, they hadn't spoken much. He had a lot to say about Brody to Savage, but Brody didn't care. He knew the decision he had was right and wasn't going back to that life.

"You looking for me?" Big Head turned to his left and sized Brody up and down. Kamren started to get nervous. By the way Big Head was sizing Brody, something bad was bound to happen.

Big Head reminded Kamren of the bald head detective from the movie Menace to Society. He always had a I don't give a fuck attitude sitting on his shoulders like a pet parrot. Kamren could admit, Brody had a few ruthless ways, but Big Head was ruthless on a higher level. He didn't have any picks on who he would jack. Kamren once overheard him say the only people he wouldn't rob was his mom and grandmother. From that day on, she never trusted Big Head. He was her least favorite out of all Brody's friends and the one she knew would turn on him.

"Yea, I'm sorry I'm late, Junior spilled milk on my white Ones," Big Head chuckled, and reached to dap Brody. Brody shook his head and said, "Junior is the only person I know that can waste peanut butter." Big Head and Brody laughed, but Kamren didn't. She stood next to Brody with her arms folded across her chest and tapping her heel against the floor. She was patiently waiting for Brody to end the conversation and walk into the church with her.

"Hell yea, he gets that from his mama side. How does she look?"

"She looks like herself, just a little swollen." Brody said.

"Damn, I don't know if I can handle seeing her like that."

"I'll let you two talk alone, but don't take too long," Kamren kissed Brody on the cheek walking away.

"I guess she's mad at me for some reason."

"You know how women are and especially Kamren." Brody said.

Brody and Big Head stood in silence until Big Head asked if True Love and Savage were in there.

"Yea, they're sitting behind my mom. She's still taking it hard, today was her first time leaving the house."

"Since it happened?" Big Head asked.

"Yea and she spends majority of the days in my sister's room. She's either crying, or going through her things."

"Damn, man, that's hard, I can only imagine what it feels like to lose a child. When Junior tells me he has a bruise or something, I'm ready to flash out. I hope your mom pulls herself together and get back to her normal self."

"I need to be the one pulling myself together and getting back to normal. My family needs me, and especially my mom. I never seen her so emotional before. This shit is fucking with my head, bruh, I don't know what to do."

"All you can do, B, is be strong. You know the saying, 'if you weak, you beat.' Just because you been out of the game, doesn't mean anything. Them niggas in the street don't know that. They probably wouldn't take you serious if you told them you were done. People still want your head on a platter, so BE careful. We can't afford to take another lost." Big Head said. Brody hated to admit it, but everything Big Head said was true. He had to find a way out of his emotions, fast. If the wrong person caught him in this venerable mind state, they would make Brody replay them for all the bad he did.

"I'm shaking back, son, I be damn if they catch me slipping. It hasn't happened before, and it won't happen now." Brody said.

"I like the way that sounds, now let's go in this church and get it over with," Big Head smiled, and placed his arm around Brody's neck. He opened the heavy doors and they walked into the church just in time. The choir was singing and they had everyone crying. Brody could feel the chills forming all over his body. He didn't realize that tears were falling down his face. He leaned against Big Head's shoulder and cried.

Kamren was also crying, but she ran to her boyfriend's side.

"Brody, I'm here for you, baby," Kamren wiped her nose and held Brody tight to her body. She could feel he was falling to the ground, she didn't know what to do.

"I should have been there, Kamren, I should have been there."

Chapter 8

Everyone sat at the large table in the Cotton's home. The old antique table was covered with dishes of food and glasses full of various drinks. Tonight, everyone was saying their goodbyes to Brody and Kamren. Even Tyson and his sisters were at the table, enjoying themselves. Joe' Ann was a chocolate bunny, with high cheekbones and long legs. Everyone was mesmerized by her height and perfect facial features. She seemed quiet, she didn't say too much. Maybe because she was around a bunch of people she didn't know. Elizabeth, on the other hand, was different. She fit right in and wasn't afraid to be comfortable.

"Oh, my goodness, Mrs. Cotton, your okra is delicious. I wish my mom could cook good like this," Elizabeth covered her mouth, that was full of food. Patty's okra had her taste buds jumping through the roof. Gravy slipped out the corners of her wide mouth and she wiped it away. She didn't want to seem like a greedy pig, but she couldn't stop eating the delicious food that covered the table. The first chance she would get, she was going to stuff some of the fresh dinner rolls into her purse for later. She prayed no one would catch her stealing and make fun of her. Being a thief wasn't the first impression she wanted to give off.

"Thank you, sweetheart, I'll make sure to fix you a to go plate. My husband and I can't eat these leftovers by ourselves." She smiled.

"Thank you, I appreciate that, no fast food tonight for me." She laughed.

"I can sense you don't get home cooked meals often." Mrs. Cotton laughed.

"Your senses are right, the cashiers at Wendy's know me by my first name."

"Damn, I can't tell you the last time I ate from Wendy's," Brody shook his head and raised his thin eyebrows. Then he grabbed a bread roll and pulled it apart. He covered the top of the bread with gravy and shoved it into his mouth. Elizabeth took a gulp of her drink and said, "well I can tell you the last time I ate there, it was yesterday," Elizabeth shrugged her shoulders and laughed. The Cottons were a little above middle class, but she didn't feel that she sounded like a hood rat when speaking to them. For the first time in a while, she was enjoying being surrounded by good conversation and great people.

"Hey, nothing is wrong with that. You have to get it how you live sometime." Brody said.

"Sometimes, you have to hustle with your muscle," Savage dropped his fork on his plate and began to flex. As his bicep went up and down, so did Valerie's eyes. Savage locked eyes with her and laughed, but no one noticed. She quickly dropped her head and continued eating. She prayed that Tyson didn't catch the sweet smile that Savage gave her.

"You got that right, my brother." Brody laughed.

"Joe' Ann, you've been quiet since you got here. Is everything okay, sweetheart?" Mrs. Cotton asked.

. "Yes, ma'am, everything is fine. This whole eating at a table like a family is new to me. I'm sorry if I'm giving off a bad vibe or anything."

"Really?" Brody asked.

"Really what?" Jo' Ann asked.

"Eating at a table like a 'family,' is new to you?"

"Yea, my sister is weird, but crazy, if you ask me. Since I was little, everyone has done their own thing. My sister and I always ate take out or had dinner with friends. Their families were just as dysfunctional as mines. I don't remember us ever owning a kitchen table." She laughed.

"That's crazy, I couldn't imagine life without Saturday dinners." Gary laughed.

"I know, I look forward to mom's potato pie every Sunday." Brody agreed.

"I must agree, I make the BEST sweet potato pie. One day, you should stop by, and I'll bake you a pie. I'm sure your sister over there wouldn't mind." Patty interrupted.

"I sure wouldn't mind, I'll be back for Sunday dinner." She laughed.

"You would do that for me, Mrs. Patty?" Joe' Ann was a little surprised at how everyone was being nice to a complete stranger. She only met Patty an hour ago and she was inviting Joe' Ann to her home already. Patty was old school and always welcomed everyone with open arms.

"Of course, I would do that, you're family now. It doesn't matter what happened in the past. My family and I will never look at you, Tyson, or Elizabeth, differently, because of what your parents did. Everyone has made mistakes, but what matters is how you fix your mistake."

"Thank you, Mrs. Cotton, and I mean that." Joe' Ann smiled, and continued to eat her food. At first, she felt awkward at the dinner table. She wasn't sure how everyone would react to her and Elizabeth, but everyone treated them as family.

"What if our dad doesn't fix his mistake?" Tyson asked.

"Don't worry, Tyson, your dad will fix this mess. The man I know is a good man, okay?" Patty said.

"I hear you, Mrs. P." Tyson replied.

"Have some faith, Tyson, just a little."

"I try to, but I want to say thank y'all also. Inviting us here means something special to me. Despite what my family is currently going through, my sisters get to be a part of real love." Tyson smiled and said.

"That's true, but things happen for a reason. We'll let the past be the past and focus on the present and future. Most importantly, our futures, because everyone in this house…. Is destined for greatness." Janice said. Her soft voice, and kind words, made everyone feel better about themselves. She wasn't one to judge others because she had a past herself.

"You're right about that. Let's make a toast to the past and the future," Tyson raised his glass in the air, and everyone did the same. They shouted out, "cheers," and tapped their glasses together. Everyone took several sips of their drinks and talked out amongst one another. Elizabeth leaned to the side and whispered into Tyson's ear. He nodded his head, then she stood to her feet.

"I want to make another toast, if you guys don't mind. This toast is for Brody and Kamren's big move, congratulations again, you guys." Elizabeth stated, and everyone raised their glasses higher in the air. Janice raised her finger in mid-air and grabbed her dinner napkin. She patted her wet eyes and took another sip of her drink.

Since the day Kamren told her mom about the big move, she cried. Kamren was sad and didn't want to leave her mom, but that wasn't going to stop her from moving.

"Mom, can you pass me the yams?" Kamren asked.

"Yes, baby," Janice grabbed the white dish and passed it to Kamren. Within seconds, she burst into tears. Kamren flared her nose rolled her eyes.

"Mom, please, enough, you shouldn't have tears left." Kamren laughed, and scooped a small portion of the yams onto her plate. She tried to ignore her mom by eating, but she couldn't. Kamren loudly exhaled and dropped her fork. She watched as her mother cried, but she couldn't stop eyeing the yams. They were juicy, flavorful, full of spices, and calling her name. She didn't want to be rude, but she slowly reached for her fork and stabbed a few yams onto it.

"Since a kid, you loved my yams. For Christmas and Thanksgiving, I would make a separate batch, just for you. One year, for Christmas, we left Santa yams, instead of chocolate chip cookies. Do you remember that, Kamren?"

"Yes, Mom, I remember, I was six years old that year. You and I stayed up until 3:00 am, but Dad was in bed sleeping by 9:15 pm. I remember that day like yesterday, I got everything that I begged for all year." She laughed.

"Yep, that's exactly what happened. If I could turn back the hands of time I would, seriously. I can't believe my baby girl is moving away."

"Once again, Mom, it's not going forever. It's only a temporary move, no longer than a year, but no less than six months."

"We're going to visit at least three times, major holidays. Before you know it, we'll be back home." Brody said.

"I know, but it won't be the same! Every morning, Kamren calls me and tells me good morning."

"Mom, I'm not sure if you know this, but I can still call you when I'm there." She laughed.

"I know, baby, but who am I going to give save my leftovers for?" Janice asked.

"Don't worry, Mrs. Janice, I'll take care of that department." Elizabeth said and laughed.

"See, Mom, you have nothing to worry about. If Elizabeth eats like me, the pots will be licked clean." Kamren laughed.

While everyone conversed, Brody sat quietly, picking at his food. He was excited about making his big announcement, but he was also scared. Kamren glanced at Brody's plate and noticed he hadn't eaten much of his food. She dropped her fork and asked, "baby, is something wrong? You're awfully quiet, and you hardly touched your food. My mother will kill you if see notices your full plate," Kamren leaned against Brody and hid her face to laugh. Her rubbed her upper thigh and laughed as well.

"No, I'm good, I'm just enjoying everyone's company. I'm going to miss these clowns, for real." Brody said.

"I know, it's going to be weird to not see them every day. I'm not trying to make any friends in Kansas. You are enough friends for me."

"Don't speak too fast, Savage is coming to Arkansas in two weeks." Brody said.

"Oh really? That's good. At least we'll have a familiar face down there." Kamren said.

"I know and he's staying for a week. He needs a break from this town. I know you hear his name ringing in the streets like a bell."

"Trust me, I do, and I'm glad he came to our dinner. He could have been anywhere else, but he's here with us. I guess we know who your real friends, or should I say FRIEND, IS," Kamren twirled her fork at the two empty chairs and shrugged her shoulders. The two empty chairs were for Big Head and True Love, but they never showed up. Since Brody said he wanted to get out of the game, the tension between the three of them were thick and heavy. Sometimes, he wasn't sure if they were his associates, friends, or enemies.

"I guess you out grow people when you use your common sense. I'm glad they didn't come, you know my mom hates them. She would have given them evil eyes and the stank face the entire time." Brody chuckled.

"I thought your mom was going throw them out of the funeral." Kamren whispered, and took a small bit of her bread. Brody stretched his eyes and smirked. That meant he thought the same thing, and he wouldn't have minded his mom throwing his 'friends,' out of the church.

"I thought she was as well. It crazy how this is how the truth was exposed. I think it's time to tell the truth about something else." He smiled.

"Go head, baby, do your thing," Kamren quickly kissed Brody on the cheek and smiled. Brody grabbed the bottle of wine and filled his glass halfway. He wasn't much of a drinker, but tonight, he had a reason to drink. As he stood to his feet, he sipped on his red wine. It was a little tart, but he brushed it off, and took another sip.

"Excuse me, everyone, I have an announcement to make."

"What is it, Brody?" Gary asked.

"Kamren, are you pregnant?" Janice smiled and asked.

"I am not pregnant, Mom, but thanks for asking me that in front of everyone," Kamren squinted her big eyes, and gave her mom a fake smile. She imitated Kamren, and they both laughed.

"This announcement is about me, well, Kamren and I, because she's going to be by my side, the entire time. For the next Saint Landry Parish election, I'm going to run for mayor," Brody placed his glass on the table and smiled. His smile and chest were huge, he felt like he was on top of the world. Kamren giggled, and held Brody's hand, she couldn't express how proud she was of Brody. Since his sister's death, she hadn't seen that smile much. At any cost, she was going to make sure it never felt again.

"Brody, are you serious?" Valerie asked.

"Yea, it's time for me to chase my dream and make my grandfather proud. Moving to Arkansas is going to clean me up and get my life together before the election."

"That's wonderful news, Brody, I'm proud of you. You're going to make your grandfather proud. Let his soul rest in peace, Brody Senior was a great man. He was a damn good mayor also, he had this city running smoothly." Gary said.

"Yes, he was, Brody Senior had a great reputation. If you win the election, Brody, you know you have some big shoes to fill. Everyone is going to expect you to be the best at what you do. Are you ready to fulfill that position and those expectations?"

"I know and I'm going to try my best to be good at what I do. It kind of makes me nervous, but I have to continue his legacy." Kamren stood to her feet and smiled at Brody. Then she grabbed her wine glass and raised it into the air. She giggled, wobbled, and flipped her hair. The wine was taking a toll on her demeanor and she was feeling good.

"I want to make a toast to you, Brody. You wouldn't understand how much I am proud of you. In a matter of two months, you've changed tremendously, and that's all I asked for. I guess my nagging finally payed off, about damn time. Excuse my language, Mom and Dad, I'm sorry." Everyone laughed and clapped their hands at Kamren's toast. Kamren placed her glass on the table and gave him a big, but warm, hug. Then she kissed him repeatedly on the cheek and rubbed his back. She didn't want to show affection in front of everyone, but she couldn't control herself. The way she was feeling right now, she had to show Brody major love.

"Thank you, baby, I'm glad I'm making you proud." Brody was feeling great, but he couldn't stop looking at the empty chairs. He thought of True Love and Big Head, then he slightly shook his head. He guessed robbing someone from Duson, Louisiana, was more important to them. On the bright side, Savage was there, and that's all that mattered.

"Since Kam is making announcements, I have one of my own. Thanks to Brody, who has inspired me, I'm going to also chase my dream. I'm going to pursue my dream in photography."

"That's terrific, Brandon, and congrats to you!" Janice cheered, and everyone clapped. The way everyone cheered him on, it made him feel good about the changes he was making. He wasn't making big changes like Brody, but he had to start somewhere.

"Brandon, that is great news. You and Brody have made some terrific announcements. Gosh, I am so proud of you two." Patty said.

"I am as well, guys, y'all are making major moves. We're going to support you two a hundred percent, believe that," Valerie smiled, and tilted her glass at Savage. He smirked and nodded his head at her. Kamren felt a strong, but positive vibe between the two. She laughed to herself because Valerie's glossy eyes told her she was drunk or tipsy. Valerie was staring at Savage as if she wanted to lie him across the table and cover him in warm gravy. Kamren couldn't wait to speak to Valerie about her innocent flirty with Savage. A few years back, Savage said he had a crush on Valerie, but she always shut him down. Savage was too street for her and she wasn't attracted to street guys, at all. If Kamren wasn't mistaking the vibe, it seemed like tonight, Valerie was liking the hood in Savage. She also wondered if Tyson noticed the flirting, but he was too busy waiting on his sisters, hand and foot.

"Thanks, Val, maybe you can be my muse. With a body, face, and smile, like yours, I'll blow up in no time. Don't worry, I won't forget about you when I do blow up." He laughed.

"You'll have to promise me to take me everywhere you go. I'm trying to be in all the blogs, as soon as possible." She giggled.

"That's a bet, Val." He smiled.

"Have you told your parents about this, Brandon?" Patty asked.

"Yes, ma'am, and my mom nearly fainted."

"Wow, don't kill Betty, you haven't given her grandkids yet." She laughed.

"I won't kill her and I'm working on the grandkids part. Hopefully, within the next year or two, I'll met a nice young woman. Then I'll give my parents ten grandkids." He laughed.

"Ten grandkids, wow, someone's back will be in pain and someone will be putting in a lot of work."

"Hey, I'm okay with putting a little work in for something I want. I'm only worried about if her head is on her shoulders correctly. A pretty face and nice body can only impress me for a short period of time." He chuckled.

"Oh, really? I'm surprised to her that coming from you, Brandon." Valerie.

"Why are you surprised, Valerie?" Savage asked.

"Uuummmm, hhmmm, your name is Savage." She chuckled.

"Just because my name is Savage doesn't mean I don't have morals and standards." He smirked, but he felt insulted. He didn't like that Valerie judged him because his name, but he played it cool. He wasn't going to let her ruin, or put a damper on, his night.

"Hhmm, I like that, and cheers to you," Valerie slid her glass across the table and gently tapped Savage's glass. She didn't say a word, but her eyes and smile told Savage enough. She wanted him, or she was doing some harmless flirting.

At this point, Valerie didn't care if Tyson was sitting next to her. His body was completely turned away from her and he was talking to his sisters. Valerie shook her head and began to eat again. She loved that Tyson's relationship with his sisters were growing, but it had its downside to it. Tyson didn't see it, but he was slowly neglecting their relationship, and her. Valerie wasn't sure how to tell him or if she should even mention it to him.

"Do you see this?" Kamren discreetly whispered to Brody, but he didn't hear her. She smacked her lips and nudged him in his hip. Brody dropped his fork and turned to Kamren. She glanced and Savage, then she glanced at Valerie. Since her head was down, she didn't notice Savage hadn't taken his eyes off her.

Brody was confused, he stared at Kamren with a blank look and waiting for answers. Kamren rolled her eyes and tossed her head backwards.

"You're the person who may run the city though, pray for us. Val and Savage are flirting at the table, how can you not see it?" She whispered.

"What?" He whispered back.

"Yes, look at Savage, he hasn't taken his eyes off her." Brody and Kamren glanced at Savage and in fact, he was staring at Valerie again. This time, she noticed and stared back. She tried to hide her with her hand, but she couldn't. It was too wide and big, Brody was shocked. Valerie always turned Savage down, he couldn't believe what he was seeing.

"Valerie looks drunk, it's probably the wine. She had about three glasses already." He laughed and shook his head.

"Her eyes are glossy, but that isn't only because of the wine."

"She's Valerie and she's probably just playing with him. Her boyfriend is sitting right there, you know she doesn't get down like that." Brody said.

"I don't know, but it's cute though, it's like puppy love."

As everyone talked, Brody became quiet again. Making that announcement had him floating in his childhood memories. In his mind, he pictured his grandfather at the table, with a big smile on his face. He was clean as a whistle in his black Giorgio Armani wool tuxedo suit. His thick salt and pepper mustache covered his top lip, but he could still see the wide smile. His blue veins also showed through his pale light skin, but he also told Brody that was because his wife would nag him so much.

Brody Senior was a wealthy man back in his day and liked the finer things. For a man his age, he wasn't big on jewelry. Brody had habit for something else and it was Italian made suits. He had a large variety of suits consisting of black, different shades of browns, blues, and grays. While his grandfather was away handling business in the town, Brody would sneak into his closet and play dress up with grandfather's belongings. Sometimes, his grandmother caught him and helped him out. They both knew if Brody Senior caught them, he would freak out.

Brody sat on the tan fuzzy carpet in his grandfather's home office entertaining himself. The small section his grandfather had him in was surrounded by toys and hand-held video games he recently purchased for him. Brody Senior had a busy schedule today and he was already running behind time. He needed Brody to stay quiet and occupy himself while he finished his notes for his speech.

At 3:00 pm, he had a press conference meeting at the city hall. He had to discuss the latest homicide shooting that took place last Tuesday night and ways to get the community involved with stopping gang violence. A seventeen-year-old girl was found beaten and murdered three blocks from her parent's home. The previous night, her parents reported her missing, but the officers told her not to worry. Unfortunately, a body was spotted, and found, by a jogger at 5: 45 am the next morning. A horrifying smell came from the bushes and she had to see what was causing the smell. She thought it was a dead raccoon or maybe a dead dog. What she found was a dismembered and discolored body, with a huge purple bruise on the chest. The face wasn't recognizable, and the chin was bashed in. Since the private area was exposed, the jogger could tell it was a girl.

Brody was only eight, and he didn't fully understand what the purpose of a press conference was. He didn't care, and the lack of knowledge couldn't keep him from being with his grandfather. He loved seeing his grandfather in action and taking pride in his career. It didn't matter how many inappropriate questions the news reporters asked, Brody Senior never broke a sweat. Rude reporters and journalist would blame him for the city's increased crime rate, but her never folded under pressure. Since Brody the second had a mild temper, he admired his grandfather for always staying calm.

"Brody." Brody Senior called out his grandson's name, but he didn't take his eyes off the paper. Brody dropped his toy truck and stood to his feet. He raced to Brody Senior's desk and said, "yes, Papa?"

"Are you hungry? I think it's time we get a bite to eat."

"Yes sir, I'm starving. Can we get fried chicken and French fries?" Brody asked.

"We can get whatever you want. Just give me a few more minutes and I'll be done," Brody Senior stroked the

trimmed whiskers on his beard and removed the thin glasses from his face. He rubbed his tired eyes and continued signing the papers. Brody stood on his tip toes to get a clearer view of what was on the papers. He couldn't see much, but he was still curious to find out.

"Papa, why are you signing those papers?"

"I have to approve the new budget cuts we are making at the parish police station."

"Why?" Brody asked.

"Because $40,000 has be stolen and wasted on nonsense. Then I have to investigate how this large amount of money has been stolen and who stole it.

"Okay, but why would someone want to steal the money?" Brody asked.

"Because they didn't think anyone would noticed the money was missing. Throughout the months, or maybe years, they have stolen small amounts at a time."

The office was spacious, but not much sunny light could enter the room. It was only two windows and they were small. Brody Senior was a private man and didn't want anyone snooping in his windows. His home office held important information about the town, budgets, and important documents. He couldn't afford anyone getting ahold of the information and ruining his reputation.

"I hope that doesn't happen to me when I become mayor."

"Oh yea, is that so?" Brody Senior asked.

"Yep and if they do, I'm going to beat them up, Papa."

"I wish it was that simple, Brody. Do you really want to be mayor, or you tell Papa that because I always buy you chicken wings?" He asked and laughed.

"No, Papa, I really want to be the mayor. I want to be just like you when I grow up."

"So, if I would be a chef, would you want to be a chef?" He asked.

"Yes, Papa, you make me proud and I love you." Brody said.

"I'm glad to know I'm making someone proud and I love you too," Brody Senior kissed Brody on the forehead and placed his glasses back onto his face.

"You do, Papa, and I don't know what I would do without you."

"You are in a good mood today, is it because of the things I brought you?" He laughed.

"No, well kind of, but I just like spending time with you. Daddy is always shouting at mom, and I don't like," Brody Senior's mouth slightly fell open and he turned to face Brody again. He pulled the glasses off his face and said, "what?"

"Uh-huh, last night he was shouting at her and he almost hit her. My mom covered her face and fell to the floor to cry. Then my dad kicked her and ran out of the house."

"Oh my God, Brody, I'm sorry you had to see that," Brody Senior grabbed Brody by the waistline, and sat him on his lap. He exhaled a little and shook his head. This was the third time this month Brody told his grandfather about the arguing between his parents. He wanted to say something, but he promised Brody he wouldn't say anything.

"It's okay, Papa, but can I tell you something else?"
He asked.

"What is it, did he hit you?" Brody asked.

"No, sir, he didn't, but I don't like him."

"I know the feeling, I don't like him either, but you
have to respect your father." He said.

"Why?" Brody asked.

"Because you won't get far in life by disrespecting
your parents. I know it's tough, but you don't want to shorten
your days because of him, right?"

"Right, but did my dad ever disrespect you as a kid?"
Brody asked.

"Sometimes, he did, but not enough. Every now, and
then, he got out of line with his mom when I was away. Let
me tell you something else, Brody, and I want you to always
remember this."

"What is it, Papa?"

"One thing you never do is disrespect a woman, any
woman! You should never make a woman feel the way your
father makes your mom feel. Damaging a woman emotionally
can come back on you ten times harder, trust me, I know."

"How do you know?"

"I know because I've hurt a few women before, but
I'm not proud of it. I was young and foolish back in my day,
but that isn't an excuse for the way I treated women."

After three hours of eating, drinking, and
laughing, everyone left the home. The only people
who were still at the Cotton's residence, were Brody,
Valerie, and Kamren. Patty was upstairs taking a

shower, while Brody and his dad were watching the game. They hated both teams that were playing, but they still chose a side and cheered the teams on.

Since Mrs. Patty was upstairs, Kamren decided to wash the dishes. Valerie stood next to her, scraping the left overs food into plastic storage containers.

"What time are y'all leaving for the airport?" Valerie asked.

"We're leaving at 10:00 am, but hopefully, the airport isn't crowded. I'm in no mood to argue with anyone over seats and luggage."

"I wish I could go to the airport with you guys, but I can't. I'm going to miss you, Kam, I kind of hate that you're leaving," Valerie placed the plastic lid on the container and pouted her skinny lips. She walked over to the icebox and slid the container on the first rack with the other leftovers. Then, Valerie closed the icebox and instantly, began to sob. Kamren wasn't sure if it was the wine that had Valerie emotional, but a single tear didn't fall from her eyes. Kamren tried not to laugh, but she couldn't help it.

"Don't cry, Val, you're going to make me cry," Kamren tossed the wet dish towel into the sink and rushed to Valerie. Her arms were wide open, and Valerie walked into her arms for a hug.

"I know, but it's going to be weird not having you here. Don't get me wrong, I'm excited that you guys are doing something good though. We've done everything together and now that's going to change, starting tomorrow."

"With the way that Joe'Ann and Elizabeth are around, they're going to replace me in a heartbeat." Kamren tried to make Valerie laugh, but it didn't work. Instead, she rolled her eyes and wiped her runny nose.

"Ugh, not at all."

"What's with the 'ugh?' I thought you liked them?" Kamren asked.

"I do, but now Tyson is spending all his time with them. When I'm in the room and they are home, he doesn't even notice my presence. For a moment, I thought they were having a threesome." She chuckled.

"Ewww, that would be disgusting and illegal. You should happy about this, it keeps him out of your face."

"I guess so, but it makes me kind of jealous." Valerie said.

"Tyson would have been jealous if he saw you flirting with Savage," Kamren titled her head forward and pouted her full lips to the side. Valerie laughed, she couldn't deny what Kamren said.

"What?"

"Girl, don't play crazy with me. I'm your best friend and I know you well. Savage didn't take his eyes off you and neither did you. Ar- are you crushing on Savage now, hhhmm?"

"Girl, that was innocent, but my point exactly. I was flirting with another guy, while sitting next to him, and he didn't notice."

"He was blind for not seeing that, but he was talking to his sisters most of the time."

"I love that he's building a relationship with his sisters, since his dad isn't trying to. I think it's mature and sweet of him, but his dad should be kissing their asses. Not Tyson, but of course, I can't tell HIM that. He's going to think I'm tripping and all that other bullshit."

"I understand what you're saying, but give it a little time. What happened between them is HUGE, and they all need to spend time together. Put yourself in Tyson's shoes, wouldn't you do the same thing?" Kamren asked.

"I probably would." Valerie said.

"Right, and look at Joe'Ann, the girl is in her thirties. Today was her first time sitting at a table and having a family dinner. Elizabeth is a firecracker just like you, y'all should get along well." Kamren laughed.

"Ugh, I hate it when you're right, Kam. Give me another hug, girl." Kamren and Valerie embraced one another with a hug and laughed. Tears finally fell from her eyes and Kamren wiped them away.

"I usually am," Kamren shrugged her shoulders and turned away. She searched the kitchen for the broom and she found it hidden in the corner.

"Savage was looking nice tonight. I think it was the collar shirt that did it, baby blue is his color. I'm so used to seeing him in basic ass white and black t-shirts." She laughed.

"He's growing into a man right before our eyes. There is a girl at my job who likes him, but I forgot to tell him. I'll call him and let him know, that girl ask me about him every damn day. You would think he was a celebrity or someone famous." Kamren laughed, and Valerie pretended to laugh. Talking about Savage made her heartbeat faster, and palms sweaty. The anxiety of holding back the information was killing her, and she had to tell Kamren soon.

"I don't think you should do that."

"Why not, she seems like she likes Savage a lot." Kamren said.

"You know a lot of girls like him for the wrong reasons. They are either using him for his name, street creditability, or money. It's probably a few girls out there that likes him, for HIM, you know what I'm saying?"

"No, I don't know what you're talking about. Brody has money, but he isn't a billionaire." Kamren said.

"In those bitch's eyes, he is a billionaire, a trap star billionaire. Don't be the one opening a thirst trap." She laughed.

"It's not that deep, Val, and besides, you seem concerned about his love life. Are you jealous that someone likes your crush?" She asked and laughed. Valerie flipped her ponytail and rolled her eyes.

"Hell no, I'm not, I'm only looking out for him. Savage is a friend of yours, so he's a friend of mine also."

"He's a friend you like to flirt with." Valerie laughed.

"I have a silly, little, tiny, confession, to make, and you will laugh your ass off." Valerie awkwardly laughed and tapped her nails on the countertop.

"What it is?" Kamren asked. Kamren began to sweep the kitchen while she waited for Valerie to respond. Valerie didn't know what to say, but she knew Kamren would be extra dramatic.

"Maannnn, when I say you are going to laugh, because I laughed also." She said.

"Are you going to tell me or leave me in suspense?" She asked.

"You know every now and then I like to smoke a little weed."

"Yea, so what?"

"Weeelllll, when I thought Tyson was cheating on me, I was smoking a lot of weed. We all know who has the best purple in town." Valerie said.

"Yep, and that is Savage, of course."

"While Tyson was away, I called Savage to the house so he could sell me something. We started talking, I offered him a plate of spaghetti, he got comfortable, and we-"

"You did what, did you two have sex?" Kamren dropped the broom and rushed to Valerie. Valerie closed her eyes and said, "no, we didn't have sex that day, but we did kiss."

"OMG, WHAT?????"

"We kissed, a big, fat, kiss, I guess his conversation turned me on."

"I can't believe you, Valerie, omg! While you thought Tyson was cheating on you, you were the one cheating on him." Kamren snapped.

"Wait a minute, Kam, I 'cheated,' but I'm not cheating on him. It is a big difference and you know that, it was only a kiss." Valerie said.

"I'm sorry to say this, but I didn't feel bad then, and don't feel bad now. Tyson had me stressing badly, and my mind was everywhere. It's not like Tyson hasn't cheated on me before. You probably need four sets of hands to count how many times I cried to you about his cheating." Valerie said.

"I understand that, Val, but you don't fight fire with fire."

"I wasn't trying to fight fire with fire, Kamren, believe me. The kiss really happened and it's on. All these years, I've misjudged Brandon, and only looked at him as a thug. Unlike Tyson, we talked about things that mattered." She said.

"Is that why you two were flirting tonight?" Kamren squealed.

"Yea, that's why, and I also feel stupid." She said.

"Why, it was only a kiss, like YOU said, Valerie. It's not like you two had sex or anything," Kamren slapped her thighs and stretched her arm to the floor and grab the broom. Valerie grabbed the broom and sighed, she had more to tell her friend.

"Do you remember when Tyson cheated on me a year ago?" Valerie chuckled and wiped her sweaty hands on the dress. Kamren nodded her head and said, "I wish I didn't remember, you were hurt, and you stayed high to numb your pain. He cheated on you with what's her face, Nevada, right?"

"Yea, it was that skinny bitch, but anyways. One night, I was lonely, and crying, when he came over. We started talking, and before I knew it, I was crying to him about my cheating boyfriend. After that, I was doing a split on my treadmill, while bouncing on Savage's dick. Let me be the first to say this…. Brandon has a BIG dick. I mean, A BIG, WIDE, FAT, JUICY, DICK." Kamren dropped the broom again and gasped. Valerie leaned against the fridge and she started to rub her thighs. Replaying how Savage gripped her thighs and stroked his dick made chills run down her spine. She was a taken woman and she knew her thoughts were wrong. She couldn't help herself or control her thoughts, savage laid the pipe down. She wouldn't admit it to him, but his sex game was official, Tyson couldn't compare.

"What the hell am I listening to?! Are you serious right now, and have you told Tyson about this?"

"Fuck no, I haven't told Tyson I cheated on him!! Would you tell Brody you cheated on him?" She asked.

"I'm not crazy enough to cheat on him, but it's clear you're crazy enough to cheat on Tyson. What if he would have found out, then what would you have done?" Kamren asked.

"I would have rubbed it in his face and he would have charged it to the game!!! That sex was waaayyyyy better than that kiss, and any sex I have had with Tyson. I swear, girl, if I close my eyes just right, I can still feel his big dick slowly going in and out of me," Valerie smiled and slapped her ass.

"That's fighting fire with fire!" Kamren snapped.

"I didn't and that's all that matters. Can you imagine how many females have had this conversation about my man?" Valerie asked.

"I hate to say this, but probably plenty females. Are we done talking about Savage and his big dick?" She laughed. "I'm ready to kick back and wait for this game to be over. My bed is calling my name, but Brody is acting like we don't have to be up early in the morning." Since Valerie didn't reply, Kamren chucked her the deuces and turned away. As she walked out of the kitchen, Valerie pulled her dress down and walked behind her. Kamren stopped and stomped her feet. Valerie grabbed her hand and said, "wait, Kam, I'm not done talking to you."

"If you're going to tell me another sexual story, I think I'll pass."

"I wish I could, but we only had sex that one time. Once Tyson came crawling back to me, I kind of pretended like it didn't happen. I told him it couldn't happen again and said he was cool with that. That kiss happened, but I hurried to stop him. He left so fast, I forgot to pay him his money. I hadn't spoken to him since then, and today, was my first time seeing him. I felt so stupid sitting at that table with him and Tyson. I know he thinks that I took Tyson back even though he cheated on me."

"He didn't cheat on you, so you shouldn't feel stupid." Kamren said.

"I know I shouldn't feel stupid, but Savage doesn't know that. Once everyone left, I called him back, so we can talk about this. Brandon and I can't do anything EVVVEERRR again, I love Tyson." The doorbell began to ring and they both turned to the door.

"I'll get the door." Kamren shouted, so everyone could hear her.

"Okay." Brody shouted back.

"Hold on a second, was he in a relationship while you two mad sex?!! I know damn well you are not a home wrecker!!"

"Fuck no, Kamren, you know I don't get down like that. However, they were together when we kissed, but that's why I stopped the kiss. I never want someone to feel how Tyson has made me feel in the past. That shit felt like pressure on my chest."

"This conversation is officially over, now let me get the door." She said and walked away.

"I'll get it, it's probably Brandon for me." Valerie wanted to smile, but she knew it would piss Kamren off more.

Valerie followed behind her and ran to the door. Before opening the door, she looked into the mirror to check her hair and teeth. Her ponytail was still slick and tight, and her teeth was free of lipstick smudges.

She opened the door, and Savage stood there with his hands in his pockets. Before Brody could see him, she stepped outside and closed the door.

"Hey." He said.

"Hi, I'm glad you came back so we can talk." She said.

"It wasn't a problem to come back here. I wasn't doing anything at home, but what's up?"

"I wanted to talk about the kiss the other day." She said.

"Oh, that's what you want to talk about?" He asked.

"Yea, what did you think I wanted to talk about?"

"I'm really not sure, but what about it?"

"Well, for starters, that can't happen again, we're both in a relationship." She said.

"That is true, but I was faithful to my girlfriend. Your boyfriend wasn't faithful to you."

"What do you mean WAS faithful to your girlfriend?" She asked.

"I mean, she WAS my girlfriend, as in the past tense. We broke up and that's the end of that. I'm not with the back and fourth games."

"I'm not being nosy, but why did you two break up?" Valerie asked.

"I'm shame to admit this, but caught that bitch cheating on me. After everything I've done for her, she still cheated on me. I swear, Valerie, some females are so ungrateful. Then, the nigga she was cheating with is a bum ass nigga. I literally, caught her in the act getting fucked in a trap house. You know they didn't have sheets on the bed, nasty ass fucking on a dirty mattress." He laughed.

"Oh my God, Brandon, I'm so sorry to hear that. I'd probably snap if I caught my boyfriend fucking another woman. Anyways, I don't want to get off subject about why I called you over here. I'm pretty sure you have a wild night ahead of you." She chuckled.

"Not at all, I'm staying in tonight alone. Too bad I don't have a nice lady who can accompany my boring night." He laughed.
"Yea I bet, but we can't ever do ANYTHING again, Brandon."

"What do you mean?" He asked.

"When we had sex last year, that was a mistake. When we kissed, that was a mistake also, and we both know that."

"Okay." Savage said.

"Okay, that's all you have to say?"

"I swear, bruh, women ae crazy, when we had sex, you told me act like it never happened. I said okay and kept it pushing, got damn!"

"Brandon, who are you speaking to like that? I said to act like it never happened because I was beyond cloud nine and it was a mistake!" She shouted in a whisper.

"You may feel like that, but I don't feel that way. We know what else was a mistake as well, so let's talk about that."

"What else, did I miss something?" She asked.

"Clearly, you did miss something, you're still with your boyfriend, that's a mistake. If you ask me, that's the biggest mistake, but who am I to judge you?" Valerie rolled her neck and sized Savage up and down. He raised his hands to his chest and took a step back. His harsh, but true, words, offended her, and he noticed it.

"What I assumed about Tyson wasn't true and he wasn't cheating on me. Those late nights he wasn't coming home was because the situation with his sister. I'm sorry if I led you on, or made you think it would have been something else."

"If what we did was a mistake, why were you flirting with me at the dinner table?" He asked.

"I -I – I don't know, I don't really think that was JUST flirty. I was congratulating you on your announcement, that's all."

"You know why you were flirting with me and you weren't only congratulating me. You were doing that because you want me, maybe just as bad as I want you. I don't know why you had that clown in my presence."

"He's not a clown, he's a nice guy once you get to know him." She whispered and turned away. Valerie pretended to look down the road because she couldn't face looking at him. What Savage said was the truth.

"Look, Valerie, I've always liked you, and you know that. I understand you have a boyfriend, so I try not to push up on you. Even though I feel like he doesn't deserve much a good woman, I still respect him. I know I wouldn't want someone all over my girl and everyone knows she taken. I respect the G code and I'm solid on stuff like that."

"Thank you for understanding, I guess. Did you tell your girlfriend about the kiss, because I haven't told Tyson?" She said.

"No, I didn't tell her, and I don't think it's any of her business now." He said.

"Good, it was only a simple and innocent kiss. It didn't mean anything to us."

"Yea, a sweet, I mean, a simple, and innocent, kiss, like this," Savage grabbed Valerie by the hips and pinned roughly pinned her against the brick wall. He knew he was a hypocrite for what he just said, but he couldn't control himself. Valerie held Savage by the face and twirled her tongue all through his mouth. Her red lipstick was smudged on his lips and face, but he didn't care. Valerie didn't want to stop kissing Savage, but she knew she had to. She gave him one more kiss, then pulled away.

"No." He whispered, and pulled Valerie back to him, but she shook her head and pushed him away.

"Brandon, stop, we can't do this."

"Why not?!"

"Because I have a boyfriend and I plan to keep it that way."

"Ffffuuuccccckkkkkkkk, be with your boyfriend, Valerie. Enjoy the rest of your night, by the way," Savage shook his head and wiped the lipstick from his lips. He took a few steps, but Valerie chased behind him and grabbed his hand. He glanced at Valerie, then he glanced at his arm. Valerie slowly released it and asked, "what is your problem and why are you talking to me like that?"

"No reason, Valerie." Brody opened the front door and Valerie's heart dropped. She wasn't doing anything wrong, but she felt as if she was. She awkwardly turned around and said, "hey, y'all."

"What's up, Savage, what are you doing here?" Brody asked.

"Uumm, I was looking for my phone. I thought I left it here, but I found it." He laughed. Valerie was so embarrassed, her cheeks were fire red. With a smirk on her face and her hand on her hips, Kamren stared at Valerie. She couldn't say anything, so she stood there, quietly.

"With Val's lipstick on your face?" Brody dapped Savage down, but the red smudges across his face caught his attention. He tried to pat his cheek, but Savage dodged his hand. He didn't want to laugh, but he couldn't help it.

"I gotta go, I'll holla at you later," Savage dapped Brody and walked away.

"What kind of shit y'all have going on out here?" Brody laughed, and he walked to the car.

"Uuuhhh, nothing, I'm tipsy, and I almost fell. Thanks to Brandon, I didn't hit the pavement," Valerie rolled her eyes and turned to Kamren. Kamren licked the tip of her index finger and wiped the lipstick away. She looked at her red finger prints laughing.

"You kissed him, huh?" Kamren asked.

"He kissed me, but I didn't pull away. I know, I'm a mess and you don't have to say it."

"You are truly something else, Miss Valerie. Good night, and I'll call you in the morning."

"Okay, girl, good night," Valerie smiled and gave Kamren a hug. Once Kamren walked off, she dropped her shoulders and exhaled. Within a matter of seconds, tonight became a long night for her. One thing for sure, she was glad her night was over.

***

After driving through the city to clear his head, Savage finally made it home. For an hour, Valerie was on his mind heavily and he couldn't get her out of his head. He even drove pass her house a few times and that shit made him feel like a stalker. He couldn't help himself, something about Valerie made him want her more than before. He wasn't sure if it was the chase or the fact that she had a boyfriend. Either way, he liked it and he wasn't going to stop until he got her.

With a blunt and pack of Kool's cigarettes in his hand, Savage walked into his house. Before turning the living room light on, he kicked his Air Force Ones off and left them at the door. As he closed the door he yawned and rubbed his face. Every little thing made him think about that kiss, but he wanted to get Valerie out of his head. At least for the rest of the night he didn't want to think about her.

"I'll show her, don't worry." He smiled to himself and laughed. He walked over to his favorite recliner and sat down. He shuffled in his pocket and pulled a fat notch of money out he began to count it. He counted the money so fast, a few bills fell to the floor and he smacked his lips.

"Damn it," without looking, he patted the floor, searching for the bills. As he grabbed a few bills, he realized he was touching something. Savage grabbed the item and placed it on the arm of the recliner. He found his white denim jeans under his couch, with money stuffed into the front pockets. At first, he didn't know where the money came from. After five minutes of being in deep thought, he remembered where the money came from and he laughed. He couldn't believe he forgot about the money he jacked from Deshawn and his friend. He wasn't in need of the money, it didn't bother him that he had misplaced the jeans.

"Pussy ass nigga, Deshawn, nigga, I took your shit. You were too pussy to do anything about it." His phone started to ring, and it was Rachel, but he didn't have anything to say to her. This was her fourth time calling in twenty minutes, but she wasn't getting the big picture. Savage was on to the next girl and looking for someone to replace her.

His phone started to ring again, but this time he was aggravated. He grabbed his phone to ignore the call, but it was a text from True Love. Savage stood to his feet and unlocked the door. True Love walked into the house with a two-piece Gucci jogging suit on and smelled like he drowned himself in Gucci cologne. Savage shook his head and continued to count the money.
"True, where the hell are you going looking like a Mississippi pimp? When that girl sees this jogging suit, she will turn around and go into her house," Savage licked his fingers so he could count the money faster and easier. He looked at True Love's outfit again and laughed.

"She's going to love this outfit, bro, but if she doesn't, then fuck her. I'm a fly guy and I wear fly shit only, you dig?"

"I hear you, True, but the keys are on the table."

"Cool," True loved walked to the table and grabbed the keys. His car was at the detail shop, and he needed to borrow Savage's car for the night. Savage had two additional cars and he didn't mind True Love borrowing one. As long as he brought it back in good condition, they wouldn't have any problems.

"Any plans for tonight?" True Love asked.

"No plans at all, my brother. I'm not spending my money on a bitch for a long time. The person I do want, doesn't want me, that's crazy, huh?" He laughed.

"I thought you were done with Rachel, but I guess not." True Love said.

"That's where you're wrong. I am done with her, and she's not the woman I'm talking about." Savage said.

"Oh word, well who's this chick?"

"I'm talking about Kamren's friend, Valerie."

"What, since when, and I thought she had a boyfriend? Don't tell me you're playing boyfriend number two." True Love laughed.

"Nigga, I'm not playing boyfriend number two, but I wouldn't mind. Shawty been on my mind since we kissed a few days ago."

"Wait, when did you kiss this girl??" True Love asked.

"I kissed her outside at the dinner. She wanted to talk about the last time we kissed. One thing led to another, and we kissed. She's saying it was a mistake, that we kissed, but I don't think it was a mistake. She's feeling me, but she stuck on her boyfriend. He cheated on her a few times, but she won't leave him."

"If you want her, you know what to do."

"Get her!" They both said and laughed.

"I don't think it's going to be easy, bro. She isn't with that street shit, she likes those square niggas. I understand that's what she likes, but this is who I am."

"Don't change yourself for some stuck-up ass bitch." True Love demanded.

"Don't call her a bitch, True, she's a nice girl." Savage shouted.

"Oooouuuuu, you must really like Valerie. You're taking up for her and shit, aawww, Savage has a crush," True Love reached to pitch Savage's, but he pushed True Loves's hand away.

"I'm serious, man, she's a nice girl. You need to start respecting my future girlfriend." He laughed.

"Now you're talking crazy, but guess who I saw earlier?"

"Who?" Savage asked.

"Rachel's hoe ass, but she didn't see me. I was at the gas station and she was with her sister, Genesis. Remind me to inbox her on Twitter tomorrow, she was looking too good in those gym shorts."

"Don't even mention her name around me. I'm so glad that's over with and I can focus on myself. I have bigger plans and saving a freak hoe isn't one of my goals."

"Exactly, bro, getting this money by any means should be your only concern. Them hoes will always be around looking to be saved." He laughed.

"I'm not Superman, it's not my job to save anyone." Savage said.

"Is she still blowing you up?" He asked.

"Hell yea, and tomorrow, I'm going to change my number. She's getting on my damn nerves."

"I guess she wants that old thing back." He laughed.

"That sounds like a personal problem. She could never get it back, I had a bonfire with her clothes last night."

"Damn, Savage, y'all really done I see."

"It's only right, but where were you earlier? Everyone was asking for you at the dinner."

"I had more important things to do than sit at a table. I'll holla at B and Kam before they leave in the morning." He said.

"Yea, yea, yea, what time are you bringing my car back? If I'm sleeping, you can keep it until the morning time."

"That's even better, I'll hit you up in the morning, Savage. If you do leave out of the house, be careful out there. The cops are rolling hard on the Hill and South."

"Well thank God I live on the West, and not the Hill or the Southside."

"Since that boy was shot on Madison Street, the Hill has been extra hot."

"Hell yea, I don't answer when my licks call from that side. The last thing I need is another distributing charge on my criminal record."

"We both can agree on that, but I'm out, B," True Love dapped Savage and walked out of the house.

"Lock the door behind you, True Love." Savage shouted, and True Love turned around. Without entering the house completely, he reached inside and locked the bottom lock. Once he closed the door, Savage closed his eyes. He was sleepy and needed to take a nap. Maybe after his nap he would feel different about staying inside on a Saturday night.

POW! POW! POW! POW! POW!

SSSSSSSSCCCCCCCCCHHHHHHHHHHHHHHHHHH!!!!

The loud tire noise started Savage and he jumped. He looked around the living room, but it was too much noise outside.

"Aaaaaahhhhhhhhh, oh, no!"

"OH MY GOD, DUCK!"

"What the fuck?!"

POW! POW! POW! POW!

BOOM!

Savage held his head and dropped to the floor. It sounded as if everyone on the street was screaming and shouting. On his arms and knees, he crawled to his love seat and grabbed the .38 hand gun. He wasn't sure where the gunshots were coming from or who they intended for, but he had to be strapped. He knew the sound of an A-R 15 assault rifle from anywhere and his .38 was no match for the machine gun.

"Who was hit? Was ANYONE hit?" A man shouted in a cry.

"No, Daddy!" A little girl replied. Hearing her cry did something emotional to Savage. At 9:15 pm, a little girl shouldn't have had to answer a question like that to her father.

"Oh my God, Peterson, the guy in the black Caprice was shot. Somebody call 9-1-1, it doesn't look like he's moving." A woman cried out for help, as if she knew the unknown driver on a personal level.

"A black Caprice, wait a minute, that's might be my car. Let me see what the hell is going on outside." With his gun still in his right hand, Savage opened the door and jogged to his mailbox. He stood on his tip toes and stretched his neck to get a clear view of what was going on down the road. From his view, it didn't look like a Caprice, and he wasn't trying to find out what kind of car it was. What he did spot was a few busted house and car windows due to the bullets. A few more houses down, were people standing in their door frames, checking out the crime scene. Some had their phones against their ears, making phone calls, while others checked their property for damages. One man even grabbed a shell casing, but quickly dropped it. He ran to his wife and gave her a hug, but Savage laughed at his neighbor's stupidity.

"Dumb ass." Savage whispered. A few of the neighbors were straight nosy, and ran to the car to see the victim. Once they got a glimpse of the driver, they ran off with horrifying facial expressions.

Now Savage was tempted to jog down the road, but he didn't make a move. He wasn't sure when the cops would arrive, and he didn't want to get caught with an illegal firearm. Being a convicted felon with a firearm, he could serve some serious time in prison.

A few houses down were a crowd of people surrounding a car that crashed into a tree. The more the crowd backed away from the area, Savage's view became clear. The front of the car was totaled, because the big tree and smoke came from under the ruined hood. Bullet holes covered the driver's side of the car and all the window was shattered. He squinted his eyes tighter and concentrated, but his eyes had to be playing a trick on him. What he was looking at couldn't be real or possible.

"No, no, no, no, no!" Savage began to panic. He rushed to hide his gun into his mailbox and dug into his pocket for his cellphone. Then he remembered his cellphone fell to the floor when he ducked for cover. Just as he started to run in his home, several cops and ambulance sped down the street. Savage was confused, he wasn't sure which direction to run to.

His legs and hands were shaking as he slowly walked to the car. He could see that the driver was leaning against the steering wheel with his eyes wide open. His body didn't move once, but blood was oozing from everywhere. A portion of his head was missing, and his brains were hanging out the back of his head. Savage felt his chest closing in and he fumbled to his knees.

"TRUE LOVE, NNNNOOOOOOOOOOOOO!" Savage cried out, in a high-pitched voice. He never cried like this before, but he had every right to. He slammed his opened hands on the concrete over and over.

"OH MY GOD," an elderly Caucasian woman pointed at Savage and covered her mouth. She almost fell to the ground, but her husband grabbed her. As an officer got out of his car, he stopped and ran to Savage. He tried to help him to his feet, but there wasn't any feeling in his legs.

"No, that's my friend, and he can't be dead. He just left my house a few minutes ago."

"Did you see what happened?" Officer Darryl Docks has been on the force for ten years. Throughout the city, he had a reputation for being a strict officer. He was only forty-five years old, but he's seen a lot on the job. Savage and Darryl have had a few run ins and three times he's arrested Savage on gun and drug charges. Two years ago, Officer Darryl was promoted to head detective, and every jack boy, and dope boy, celebrated. That meant the only time you would see him is for a shooting. They no longer had to worry about him patrolling the streets while they were up to no good.

"I didn't see what happened, because I was in my house. I heard gun shots, what sounded like a machine gun and people were screaming. Then I heard my car crash as well."

"This black car is your car?" Darryl asked.

"Yes, sir, it is.

"Why was he in your car?" Darryl asked.

"He said he was going on a date and he was going to pick her up. His car is in the shop, I let him use mines."

"Okay, that's good information, but did he tell you who the girl was?"

"No, sir, he didn't, and I didn't bother to ask him. Now I wish I would have asked him, fuck, man!"

"I'll be right back." Officer Darryl said and walked away.

 Savage sobbed harder, but he wiped his snotty nose with the sleeve of his shirt. The officer held a tight grip on Savage's arm and made him stand to his feet. Then he slowly walked to his patrol car and opened the door. He pointed to the back sit and said, "you can have a seat and collect yourself." Savage took one look at the back seat and said, "I'm fine, I can lean against the car."

"Are you sure?" The officer asked, and Savage nodded his head up and down. He knew the back seat of a cop's car too well and didn't feel comfortable sitting there. In his mind, the officer could charge him with anything, and take him to jail. Before he could answer the question, he could feel a headache striking through his head. Even though he hated to, he sat down. The commotion and sirens made him close his eyes and rubbed his temples. Everything was too much for him and he wanted to scream.

"You look a little flushed, I think you need to let one of our E.M.T.'s check you out," Officer Darryl used his notepad to point to the ambulance van and waited for Savage to stand to his feet. At first, he hesitated, but when he realized sweat dripped from his face, he stood up. He slowly walked to the ambulance truck, but his legs still felt numb. He shielded the left side of his face with his hand, because he couldn't look at the crime scene.

With everything that was going on, he forgot he needed to call Brody. He pulled his phone out and rushed to dial Brody's number, but he didn't give him a chance to say hello. Brody shouted, "B, you need to come to my house quick. True Love was shot, man, and shit not looking good. Call Big Head and y'all come quick, please!"

"What? I'm on my way." In a panic, Brody disconnected call.

Savage sat at the back of the ambulance van waiting for his friends to arrive. He tried his best to stay calm, but he couldn't. Watching the medical examiner zipped that body bag, shredded his soul into a million pieces. He couldn't take it anymore and he could feel his stomach getting weak. He jumped off the van with his hand clutch to his stomach and a mouth full of warm vomit. The after taste of yams and wine floating in his mouth, he quickly released the vomit into a bush.

"Uggghhhh." Savage groaned and held his stomach tighter. The female paramedic chased behind Savage with a cold bottle of water and patted his back. The brown skin, and clear complexion, girl, smiled at Savage and handed him the bottle of water.

"I thought you might need this." She said.

"Thanks, I appreciate it." Savage said and opencd the bottle of water. He took big gulps and swished it around his mouth. Then he released the water into the bushes and placed the cap onto the bottle. The girl smiled at Savage, but he didn't know why. Her baby face and short height made her look as if she was in her early twenties. Her badge read Karina Johnson, so Savage asked, "why are you smiling so much, Karina, do you know me?"

"I don't know you, I just like to smile." She laughed. He couldn't lie, Karina was fine as hell. She was sexy in her work uniform, but a woman was the last thing he could think about. Even though her ass was round and fat with the perfect waistline to match it.

"Oh okay, thanks for the water again." He said.

"You're more than welcome and I'm sorry about your friend." Karina said.

"Yea, me too."

"Savage, is that you?" Kamren shouted, from a distance, and Brody turned around. Vomit dripped from the side of his mouth, so he rushed to wipe it away. He waved at Kamren and she ran in his direction. Karina smiled again and walked away.

Kamren grabbed Savage by his shoulders, but he couldn't look her in the eyes. He cried through a closed mouth and shook his head. She grabbed his face and said, "Brandon, what's wrong, and why are these cops here? Why is your car wrecked, why is there blood in the inside of your car? I see blood and bullets everywhere, something isn't adding up! Please don't tell me something happened to True Love in your car, no, don't tell me that," Kamren's lips trembled, and she nervously ran her fingers through her hair. It felt like time stopped as she waited for Savage to answer her question.

"I should have been with him. What am I going to tell his mom?" He whispered.

"You should have been what? WHAT HAPPENED, BRANDON? TELL ME SOMETHING!" Kamren and Savage were startled by a loud shouting and it was Brody. Tears were falling down his face and they made Savage cry more. Kamren pointed in Brody's direction and tried yelling, but she only shuttered.

"True Love is dead, Kamren." Savage said, and dropped his head.

Chapter 9

Everyone sat in Savage's living room with faces drowned in tears and hearts full of emotions. Everyone wanted to say something, but none of their words would fix or adjust the situation.

"This cannot be real, who was True Love beefing with? How did they know he was at your house?" Kamren wiped her tears away and pulled her hair into a ponytail. Her tears made wet strains of hair stick to her neck and face and it irritated her skin. She brushed the loose hairs into her ponytail and scratched her neck.

"I don't recall him beefing with anyone." Brody said. He pulled Kamren closer to him and rested his head on her shoulder. Kamren gently rubbed his face and kissed his forehead. This was the second death Brody experienced in a short period of time and she wasn't sure if he could handle it.

"I don't think True Love was beefing with anyone, unless he didn't tell us. Whoever knew he was here, had to follow him here." Big Head said.

"It's not like him to not tell us something like that." Savage said.

"Savage, did you see who dropped him to your house? Maybe they know something that we don't know." Kamren said.

"I didn't see anyone, but he did say he was going on a date with some girl. He didn't say her name and I didn't bother asking who it was."

"I'm sure his phone holds a lot of information, but the police aren't letting that phone go anytime soon." Valerie said.

"Has anyone spoken to his parents again?" Kamren asked.

"I spoke to his dad a few minutes after they left from here. That had to rush his mom to the hospital, I guess this took a toll on her." Brody said.

"Damn, poor Mrs. Emma, I hope she's okay." Kamren said and shook her head.

"Who can blame her? I know it would have done the same to me." Valerie said. Savage rubbed the back of his head and stood to his feet. He walked into the bathroom and slammed the door. Everyone jumped, but no one said anything to him.

"Brody, I think you should talk to him." Kamren said.

"I know Savage, and I don't think that's a good idea. He needs some time to himself, to think, and gather his thoughts."

Savage stared at himself in the mirror and shook his head. He was lost and didn't know what to do with himself anymore. He turned the hot and cold water and splashed it on his face. As Savage turned the water off, he reached for a small towel and patted his face.

Then walked out of the bathroom and walked into his bathroom. In rage, he slammed his bedroom door and leaned against his door. Then he walked to his bed and laid flat on his back. He stared at the ceiling fan and thought about True Love.

"Damn, True Love." He whispered to himself. The way his eyes were opened was stuck in his eyes and he couldn't get it out.

"I'm going to talk to him." Valerie said.

"Please do, Val, you might be the only person that can calm him down." Kamren implied.

"I'll try my best, Kam," Valerie sighed and stood to her feet. She slowly walked down the hall and knocked on the door. She quickly fluffed her hair and said, "Brandon, it's me Valerie, can I come in?"

"Yea." Valerie walked into Savage's room and quietly closed the door. She leaned against the wall and her eyes wandered through the room. For a few seconds, she didn't say anything, but she knew she didn't come into his room to stand in silence. Savage stared at Valerie, but she wasn't sure what to say. In the situation, he was in, it wasn't much see could say that would make him feel better.

"I know it's stupid to ask this, but are you okay?"

"If it was stupid to ask, why did you ask me that?" Savage chuckled and motioned for Valerie to sit next to him. She nodded her head and walked to the bed. Savage didn't take his eyes off her at all. Being this close to her again made him feel good, but it made her nervous. Being in his presence, let alone his bedroom, wasn't healthy for her relationship. Valerie wasn't a fool and knew this could escalate between them at any moment.

"Because I'm not sure what to say or ask you. I can only imagine how you're feeling right now and I wish I could change that." She said.

"I feel like shit, I can't lie, Valerie. I'm trying to get a grip on life, but everything happened so fast. One minute, I was clowning his jogging suit, then the next minute, he's dead. How in the hell does that happen without me seeing it about to happen?"

"That's because you can't predict the future. I'm pretty sure if you could, you would have." Valerie said.

"Trust me, I would have, and instead of him, it would have been me in my car."

"Don't say that, Brandon, don't ever say that again!"

"It's the truth though, and no one can make me feel any different," Savage shook his head and turned away.

"If it was you, we would STILL be here crying over someone's death. I'd probably cry harder if it was you, it would fuck my head up."

"Oh really, you would cry if Big Daddy Savage died?" He asked and laughed.

"Nnnnoooo, I would cry if Brandon Barre died. That would hurt a lot, you know?"

"Well, I'm glad to know someone would be hurt if I died. Even though that same person doesn't want to give me a chance at stealing her hurt." With an easeful touch, Savage placed his hand on Valerie's chest and stared her in the eyes. It made her nervous, but what she saw in his eyes, was something she never saw in another man. Which is security and trust. Her heart started to race, so she grabbed his hand and placed it on her knee.

"I'm surprised that you're still here, but I hope your boyfriend don't come around here tripping. I would hate for it to be another homicide in this neighborhood." He said.

"Hey, that IS my boyfriend, don't talk crazy like that." She whispered.

"Well does your boyfriend even know you're here?" He asked.

"Yes, he does."

"If you knew what I did to you with my mouth, would he still be okay with you being here?" He asked and laughed.

"Oh my God, Brandon, shut up. What he doesn't know will not hurt him and I'm pretty sure he has said that about me plenty of times."

"Fuck him, you know he isn't fucking with me anyways." He smirked.

"Maybe he is, but maybe he isn't. Can I ask you a question?" Valerie asked.

"What's up, V?"

"Why do they call you Savage?"

"Well, it sure isn't because of my good ways. If that's the case, they would call me Angel." He laughed.

"Hhhmm, that's not the answer I was looking for." She laughed.

"Seriously though, they call me Savage because I do savage shit. Since a kid, I didn't take shit from anyone."

"That explains a lot."

"I guess so, but is there anything else you want to know? Like, what's my favorite color or food?" He asked and laughed.

"Well, by the looks of things, it looks like you like the color black," Valerie pointed at the black curtains, rug, and comforter set. She spotted six pairs of black tennis shoes by his dresser and pointed at them as well. Savage laughed and shrugged his shoulders.

"I guess you can say my favorite color is black, Valerie."

"That was a wild guess, seriously though, how are you feeling?"
"I'm feeling numb honestly, and I don't want to accept the truth. I think it's best that way or I will flash out. Everyone is a suspect in my eyes and I don't trust anyone."

"I understand that, Brandon, but you feel like that. I know you don't want to hear this, but this isn't your fault." Valerie said.

"How do you know that?" Savage asked.

"Because I just know that. What I said earlier doesn't dictate me being here for you in your time of need. It doesn't matter what time or day, you need ANYTHING, don't hesitate to call me."

"Thank you, Valerie, I appreciate that. I wish you could rewind time and bring him back, that would be nice." He smiled.

"Trust me, Brandon, if I could, I would do that for you in a heartbeat. I hate seeing my friend this way."

"Your friend, huh?" He asked and smiled. Valerie covered her face and laughed.

"Yes, my friend, and I don't want to lose him as my friend."

"I'm glad to know you cherish our friendship, maybe it was the kiss or the big dick. I wish you would cherish that as well."

"Brandon, you are so nasty." She laughed.

"I'm joking, baby girl, I'm just trying to keep from crying." He laughed, but Valerie pinched his arm. In a sexual manner, he grabbed her by the shoulders, and laid her across the bed. Valerie was ready to wrap her legs around his back, but she didn't.

"The last time I was like this, never mind."

"I'll finish your sentence for you, the last time you were like this, I had your legs spread apart while you laid on the floor. My face was buried deep in your pussy and I had you moaning my name. Just the way you moaned my name made my dick hard. Do you remember that, Valerie?" Savage slowly pulled her legs apart and she didn't push him away. He walked closer to her and pressed his soft penis against her vagina. He knew if they continued to play this little game, his dick would get rock hard.

Valerie held Savage's hand and stared him in his eyes. Once again, Valerie was doing something wrong, but it felt good.

"Yes, I remember that, it seems like yesterday you were inside of me. I can't lie, Brandon, you make me different, but in a good way. I wish I would have met you before I met Tyson, then I wouldn't be in this mess." She rolled her eyes and shook her head. Savage climbed on top of her and kissed her forehead. She smiled and bit her bottom lip.

"I can see it in your eyes that you aren't happy, Valerie. I know that nigga isn't fucking you right either. Let me be the one to make you happy and I promise I won't fuck up. That's my word, ma, and you can hold that against me." He said.

"It's not that easy, but I wish it was. Tyson and I have history and you know that." She said.

"I understand that, but fuck that history. We can make history of our own, think about that. Think about how I can make you happy and fuck you right. Do you know how I would please this beautiful body of yours?" He asked.
"I don't know, so how about you tell me?"

"I would slowly pull your pants off, then I would pull your panties off with my teeth. While I'm doing that, I would massage your pussy and watch your sweet juices cover my fingers. I swear, I can still taste your pussy on my lips."

"Oh yea, what else would you do, or that's it?" She asked.

"Hell no that isn't it love. Your pussy would be throbbing because the fourplay would have you begging for me. I have to make sure that pussy is dripping wet before I slide my dick in. Once I'm in, you know it's a wrap, I'm going to have you screaming my name again. You might lose your voice because you're going to be screaming so much."

Knock! Knock! Knock! Knock! Savage quietly exhaled and closed his eyes. Just when he was about to kiss Valerie, they were interrupted.

"Brandon, can you open the door? It's me."

"Rachel?" He asked.

"Your ex-girlfriend, Rachel?" She whispered and pushed him off her.

"Yea, that's her, but I'm not sure why she's here."

"I'm more than sure she's here for you, but I could be wrong. I'll let you find out and I'll call you later." Savage smacked his lips and pulled Valerie closer to him. He reached in to kiss her again, but Rachel knocked and said, "Brandon, open the door. I know you're in there." Savage dropped his head and Valerie said, "I think that's my cue to go home, Brandon." Valerie wanted to kiss Savage before she left, but she didn't. She stood to her feet and adjusted her shirt over her ass. Savage jogged to the door and opened it.

Rachel's jeans and t-shirt were covered in dust and had tiny blood stains on her shirt. Smudges of mud was on her cheek and she was bare foot. Pieces of leaves and twigs were in her head. Savage was shocked and curious to find out why she looked a mess.

"What the hell, Rachel, what happened to you?" Savage asked.

"Hey, I would like to talk to you in PRIVATE."

"Fine with me, sweetheart, and you have a great night. Brandon, call me if you need anything, okay?" Valerie said.

"Okay, Val."

Rachel mugged Valerie as she walked out of the room, but Valerie laughed and closed the door. The door was closed, but Rachel still pointed and stared at it. Savage leaned against his dresser with a tired look on his face. He wasn't in the mood to argue with Rachel and didn't understand why she was in his house or his room.

"Damn, Brandon, we've only been broken up for a few days. You already have another bitch where I laid my head at. I didn't know you rock like that."

"You've been cheating on me for how long? I didn't know THAT YOU rocked like that! Matter of fact, what do you want? You can offer your condolences for True Love over the phone." He said.

"That would have been rude and I'm way better than that. I came here to see how you were doing and to be here for you. Just because we aren't together doesn't mean I don't care," Rachel sat on the bed and pretended to cry. Instead of comforting her, he laughed. He was used of her pulling this stunt, but he wasn't falling for it this time.

"I'm still waiting for a tear to drop, quit it, Rachel."

"Whatever, Brandon." She said and wiped her dry face.

"I lost my friend a few hours ago and I'm not doing well. Thank you for checking on me, ex-girlfriend, and have a good night," Savage pointed to the door, but Rachel didn't stand to her feet.

"NO, BRANDON, I'M NOT LEAVING, AND YOU NEED TO LISTEN TO WHAT I HAVE TO SAY! Once I tell you this, I have to leave Opelousas, and probably Louisiana for good, because I will die next!"

"What the fuck do you have to say, Rachel, huh? If you want to give me an apology, don't do it."

"That's not what I came here for, I need to tell you who killed True Love and why they did it," Savage's eye stretched wide and Rachel covered her mouth. He slowly walked to the edge of his bed and stood in front of Rachel. She took one look at Savage and burst into tears. He exhaled and sat next to her. With tears runny from her hazel eyes, she dropped her head into his lap and he stroked her hair.

"Rachel, what are you talking about?" He asked.

"Brandon, I'm so sorry that this happened to True Love. Everyone knows he was a good person and he didn't deserve to die."

"Tell me what the hell you are talking about, Rachel, please! You said you know who killed him and why they did. Do you mean they, as in more than one person?" Savage asked.

"Yes, it was more than one person. Deshawn and his friends are the ones who killed True Love, but he wasn't supposed to die."

"What is his two friend's names?" Savage asked.

"One's name is Darrius, but they call him Dee Thugger. He's from New Roads, but you can catch him hanging on Madison Street. The other one name is Marquis, and he's from the Southside. Marquis is a quiet guy, I didn't know he was from here."

"Marquis has two sisters named Lynika and Heaven?" Savage asked.

"Yea, that's their names, two stuck up bitches, if you ask me. The plan was to catch YOU, coming out of your house, and shoot you. They didn't expect it to be someone else, but they kept shooting."

"Are you serious, Rachel? They wanted to kill me because of what I did Deshawn?"

"Yea, and since that day, he basically held me hostage at his grandma's house. I wasn't sure where I was, and how I got there. I think I was drugged, Savage, but he didn't want to let me leave."

"Why didn't you call someone or the police to get you?" Savage asked.

"I -I – I I'm not sure, Brandon, I guess my only concern was you. I wanted to make sure you were safe. I tried to prevent this from happening. Every time I called you, you didn't answer my calls." She said.

"Thank you for telling me this, but how did you get out the house?" He asked.

"He had his grandma watching me, but she fell asleep. I can't believe I was guarded by an eighty-year-old!! I found a little window in the basement and ran for my life. It took me about an hour to get out her house, and I found my way by the old K.C. Hall. I wanted to go to my mom's house, but I had to come here first."

"I'm glad you came here first and thank you for telling me this. Have you spoken to him since you ran away?"
"No, I haven't, but he's been calling and texting me nonstop! He's made threats about killing me when he finds me. I have this gut feeling that he's going to try and hurt Brody also."

"Why do you say that?" He asked.

"Because he said I'm going to kill THEM niggas. That's when I started calling you, man, I wish you would have answered."

"I wish I would have answered as well, all of this is my fault." Savage couldn't believe he was the reason True Love died, and he wasn't sure how everyone would take the news. On top of that, he had to figure out how he would tell Brody he was a possible target as well.

"Don't beat yourself up for this, Brandon I know how you get down, so everything is going to be okay." Rachel said.

"It's kind of hard not to."

"I know, but where are my clothes? I would love to change out of these clothes and start cooking you something," Rachel jumped to her feet and walked to the closet. When she opened the door, she was surprised to see her belongings were gone. She turned to Savage, and he said, "I burned them like on Waiting to Exhale."

"WHAT, ARE YOU SERIOUS RIGHT NOW?" She asked.

"I'm very serious right now, can you tell in my face?" Savage pointed at his slim face and shrugged his shoulders. Rachel was pissed, but she couldn't do anything about it. She took a step closer to him, but he took two steps back. Savage's careless behavior offended her, and she was ready to snap on him.

"I can't believe you." She said, as she exhaled and turned around. Rachel paced through the room to calm herself down, but it didn't work. She slammed her tight fist in her open hand and shouted, "UUUGGGHHHHHHH, I can punch you right now, Brandon Alexander Barre!!! How could you do that, you could have told me pick up my things. I guess you burned my things so that girl can move her things in?!"

"First of all, that girl is Kamren's friend. Second, she has a boyfriend name Tyson. Third, she was here to check on me, but I don't have to explain anything to you. We're both single and we can do what we want. Unlike you, I waited until after we broke up and not before."

"Brandon, you don't have to remind me of what I did. I understand you are hurt, but that was harsh." She said.

"Seeing you get fucked like a porn star was harsh, but I'm over it."

"I can't believe you just said that!" She squealed.

"You need to believe it, because that's what I saw. That nigga bent you over in ways you would refuse to let me do. It's all good though and you know I'm not pressed for pussy."

"We'll see how long it'll be before someone's pussy is in your face." She said.

"It might be tonight, or tomorrow, you never know." He laughed.

"Screw you, Brandon, and whoever you're screwing. Can you at least say you're sorry? I think you owe me that much!" Rachel shouted and pushed his head. He grabbed her hand and pushed her to the bed. Rachel wanted to swing again, but she wasn't sure if he would hit her back. Instead, she laid flat on her back and waited for her apology.

"I'm not sorry that I burned your belongings."

"What?" She rose and asked. She turned to Savage with a mean mug on her face, but his facial expression didn't change.

"I said I'm not sorry. I won't replace them either, but you can wear one of my t-shirts and shorts." Savage walked to his dresser and pulled on the gold handle. He grabbed a white t-shirt and blue shorts, then he tossed it to Rachel. The clothes fell on the bed and she shook her head.

"Wow, that's crazy, but I guess I'll charge it to the game. What do you want me to cook for you?" Rachel asked. She grabbed the shirt and pulled it over her head. Her big breasts jiggled as she moved, and Savage couldn't take his eyes off them. Rachel's breasts were always his favorite part of her body, but he wasn't going to get sidetracked by a pair of big breasts. At the end of the day, she was just another cutthroat female with a large set of breasts.

Rachel pulled her pants off and her private areas were exposed. She didn't care about Savage seeing her ass and pussy because it was once his. Rachel quickly slipped the shorts on and sat down again. Savage tried his best to keep his eyes off her pussy, but he couldn't help himself. Before she could catch him staring at her, he turned away and stared out of the window. His mind was in another place, but he still needed to check his surroundings. He didn't have a strap on him, but he kept a few machine guns under his bed and in his closet.

"I don't want you to cook me anything. After you take a shower, I'll sneak you out the house, and Big Head will drop you wherever you need to know."

"PLEASE, BRANDON, DON'T DO ME LIKE THAT! YOU HAVE TO HELP ME GET OUT OF OPELOUSAS, OR AT LEAST AWAY FROM OUR HOUSE!!! I KNOW I CHEATED ON YOU AND I'M SORRY. YOU WERE GOOD TO ME, BUT PUT THAT TO THE SIDE FOR RIGHT NOW. ONCE I'M OUT OF THIS HOUSE SAFE, I'LL BE OUT OF YOUR LIFE FOREVER." Everything that Rachel said made Savage's heart skip a beat. He hated Rachel right now, but he couldn't leave her to die because of him.

"Where do you need to go, Rachel?" He asked.

"I don't know, Brandon, maybe I can go to Port Allen. I have relatives there, but I can't stay there for long. He knows about them and that could be one of the places he looks for me. I'm going to get a bus ticket and plan my next move from there. I don't feel safe being here and I don't want to put anyone's else life in danger."

"I understand, and I got you, but first, I need to tell Brody and everyone else what's up. We can decide your next move from there, okay?" He said.

"That's cool, Brandon, and thanks a lot." Rachel said.

"No problem, but I feel like it's my fault you're in this situation. I should have never lost my temper and beat that dude. Sometimes, love can make you do crazy things."

"You know what, like a woman, I can admit that this is my fault. You were good to me and I shouldn't have cheated on you. Any woman would die to have you in her life, as a friend, or even her man. From the bottom of my heart, I'm sorry for cheating on you. None of it was worth it and Deshawn damn sure wasn't worth it."
"You say he wasn't worth it, but why did you cheat on me?" Savage was curious to know why Rachel cheated on him, but it wouldn't change anything. What she did to him cut deep and it would take time for the damages to be repaired. He loved Rachel and besides his mother, she was the only woman he cared for. Despite the petty break ups and disagreements, he wanted to be with Rachel for the rest of his life. Even though he had a minor crush on Valerie, he'd still choose Rachel.

"I don't know, honestly, Brandon. Deshawn has been in my inbox asking for my number. I would turn him down and laugh it off, but one day, I didn't. I guess it was the attention he gave me, but that still wasn't a reason to cheat on me. If the shoe was on the other foot, I don't know how I would have handled it all. I could never watch the man I love fuck someone else. I can imagine how you felt when you saw that."

"I felt like shit, I was hurt, and disappointed in you. I thought you knew better, but I guess not. Am I still hurt? Yes, I am, but only because I love you. Am I holding a grudge against you because you cheated on me? No, I'm not holding a grudge against you."

"You seem so calm and relaxed about this. I wish you were mad at me, I think that would make me feel better," Rachel laughed and wiped her tears. Savage could tell she was hurt, but that didn't change the fact that she ripped his heart into shreds.

"I have a lot on my mind and I don't have the energy to be upset with the wrong people."

Savage sat next to Rachel and rubbed his face. If he could delete today from his memory, he would in a heartbeat. She sat closer to him and leaned in for a kiss, but he swiftly pushed to the side. Rachel didn't catch his vibe, so she grabbed his place and brushed her lips against his.

"I don't think we should be doing this," Savage exhaled and stood to his feet. Rachel was confused so she stood to her feet and said, "why not? It's like we still don't love one another."

"Of course, I still love you, but I'm not feeling this. I told you I have a lot on my plate and so do you."

"I guess you're right, but I don't want to lose you, Savage. You were the best thing that happened to me and I mean that." She said.

"You'll never lose me as a friend, Rachel, I'll always be here for you." He said.

"Thanks, Brandon, I appreciate that. I'm still in shock about this, it's wrong! How could Deshawn do something like this?"

"I guess he wanted to drop his nuts today, but a cake baked for him. I'm already plotting on how to take him out this bitch."

"Please, don't get hurt in the mist of this, I would lose my mind if something happened to you."

"I got this, so chill out, baby girl. That nigga is going to wish he never drove on my street with that bullshit." He chuckled, but Rachel didn't laugh. The look in Savage's slanted eyes was too familiar and she hated it. He had the same look in his eyes when his house was robbed months ago. Once the homicide made the news, Rachel saw Savage's names written all over it. She never questioned him about it and he never said anything about it as well. Most of the times, he didn't tell her about the foul play he participated in the streets. Rachel didn't question it because the less she knew was better for her.

"What if they're still watching your house and try to shoot you again?" Rachel asked.

"Trust me, them niggas not built like that. I need to holla at Brody and Big Head," Savage pinched Rachel's cheek and walked out of the room. She held her cheek and smiled a little. It reminded her of how he would squeeze her cheeks while they were lying in bed.

She stared at every inch of the bedroom, but it made her emotional. She fought back her emotions, but she couldn't control the tears that fell from her face. Rachel didn't have a problem admitting the truth, she fucked up bad. As she heard Savage laughing and opening the door, she turned away and wiped her tears.

Savage reentered the room with Brody, Kamren, and Big Head. Brody seemed calm, but Big Head's attitude was on ten. He couldn't control how he rolled his eyes and flared his nose at her. Rachel wasn't going to say anything, but Big Head made her feel uncomfortable. Everyone stared at her and Rachel burst into tears.

"I'm sorry everyone, I feel like this is my fault. If I wouldn't have cheated on Brandon, none of this would have happened."

"NO, IF YOUR DUMBASS WOULDN'T HAVE GOTTEN CAUGHT CHEATIN, NONE OF THIS WOULD HAVE HAPPENED!" Rachel's glanced at Big Head as he paced though the room. Kamren walked behind him and punched his shoulder. His harsh words cut deep, but Rachel fought back the rest of her tears.

"He didn't mean that, Rachel." Kamren rolled her eyes and gave Rachel a hug. She hugged Kamren tighter and a few tears dropped on her shoulder.

"It's okay, girl, I'm here if you need someone to vent to." Kamren whispered into Rachel's ear, because she felt like everyone was against her.

"Yea, he meant that, and everything else that's going to come out his month. Be honest, Big Head, you NEVER liked me! I bet you're happy I'm the cause of this, now you can be up front with not liking me."

"You're right, and I'm glad I didn't have to waste my precious time saying it! From day one, I told Savage you were no good, but he didn't listen to me. I guess it was the fat ass and tight pants he couldn't get pass. If he would have listened to me from day one, we wouldn't be in this mess!"

"BIG HEAD, FUCK YOU, YOU'RE JUST MAD BECAUSE I CHOSE BRANDON AND NOT YOU! Let's be clear, you could never bag someone like me. I see those drug heads you run around town with, boy, you are hit!"

"You aren't that different from them. Let's be real, you were fucking Deshawn's broke ass. As for me wanting you, it was never that. It's a big difference between me and my nigga Savage, but you wouldn't understand." He said.

"Oh yea, what's the difference, since you know everything?" She shouted. The difference between Savage and I, is that I would have beat your stupid ass. I probably would have put a bullet in you, and all them nigga's heads. Then we wouldn't be in this shit, for real." He laughed.

"Fuck you, Big Head, and I wish it was you in Brandon's car instead of True Love!!" Rachel shouted, and this time, she couldn't fight back her tears. They streamed down her face and Big Head laughed. His laughter only pissed her off more and she raised her hand to swing at him. Before her hand could reach his face, Savage grabbed it and bear hugged her.
"Chill out, Rachel, what the hell is wrong with you?"

"HE is the problem and not me! I can't stand his ass, and on my life, I wish it was him!! I wish it was HIS MOM CRYING, AND not Terry's mom. He didn't deserve to die," Rachel dropped to the floor and sobbed. The pressure weighed on her back heavily and she didn't know how to handle it. Savage and Kamren dropped to the floor to help her stand, but she shook her head.

"Let her ass stay on the floor." Big Head said.

"HEY, YOU TWO NEED TO STOP!! What we're not going to do is play the blame game. You got that, Big Head? That's the first, and last, time, you're going to do that," Kamren's chest expanded up and down, she was pissed with Big Head. He didn't have a filter on his month and little respect for women. Kamren has witnessed Big Head disrespect women plenty of times and never said anything. This time, she couldn't bite her tongue and turn the other way. Savage ignored Rachel's request and made her to stand to her feet. She sized him up and down, but he ignored her. Savage placed her on the bed where she rocked side to side. Rachel couldn't make eye contact with anyone and was ready to put all this behind her.

"Rachel, Savage said it was the guys we beat up who did this, and I could be their next target. How much is true in what he said?" Brody asked.

"I hate to say this, but it's all true, Brody."

"Okay, so that means they were talking just to hear themselves talk. Or they about that real shit and they come for us at any moment."

"You're smart, Brody, and I don't have to tell you how this is going to turn out if y'all don't act fast."

"I know you're trying to get out the city in one piece, but you have to help us as well," Brody stared at Rachel, but she couldn't make eye contact with him. If Brody could have heard the way Deshawn spoke about his death, he would run the other way. Kamren didn't want to panic in front of everyone, but she was worried about Brody's safety. He worked hard to pull himself out the streets, and something like this, could pull him back in deeper.

"How?" She asked.

"The sooner you leave, the better. If you haven't already, you're going to have to cut ties with Deshawn, right now. Once he realizes you aren't on the scene, then he's going to know something is up." Brody said.

"Okay, then what?"

"He's going to lay low, or go harder, but either way, we have to clear that business." Brody said.

"Hell yea, and I'm talking asap, like Rocky." Savage laughed and dapped Brody.

"Well, let's put this shit in motion, you dig, I'm going to smoke a cigarette," Big Head dapped Brody and Savage up, then he walked out of the room.

"Baby, I need you to take Rachel home with you. Matter of fact, I want you to go to your parent's house tonight. I don't want you anywhere around the house by yourself."

"What? I'm staying with you. I'm not going to my parent's house, at all. If they saw the news, they are going to ask me a hundred questions!"

"No, you're not, and we can't move right now. Not until we figure all this shit out."

"What, Brody, are you serious?" Kamren questioned Brody in an upset tone. She was pissed, but right about now, Brody didn't give a fuck about that.

"Look, we'll talk about that later, but just go to your mom, baby. I love you, yea," Brody attempted to kiss Kamren on the lips, but she gave him her cheek instead and rushed out of the house, slamming the door. Exhaling loudly, Brody couldn't deal with all this drama right now. If he was the weak type, he would have folded by now because of the intense pressure. By the look of things, his future and dreams would be going down the drain seeking revenge for his friend.

"What's up with you and Valerie? Y'all were in your room for a long time." Brody laughed.

"Man, I'm trying to get with her, but she's stuck on that Tyson cat."

"You know she's not giving up the cookie that easily, use your head."

"It's not about the pussy, I already had that before. I'm trying to make her my girl, no games, you feel me?" Savage said.

"Wait, you already had the pussy? When did this happen?" Brody was shocked and couldn't stop smiling at the news he was hearing. He knew how much Savage liked Valerie and knowing he's been close to her made him feel like a proud big brother.

"Them niggas won't put us on a rest in peace shirt, Savage. I'm not going out like that, believe me."

"You down for some gangsta shit tonight? The faster we clear this business, the faster we can get back to our normal lives."

"Naw, Savage, you know we don't operate like that. We have to come correct, or this can go left if we don't. I don't need an attempted murder charge pending on my head."

Chapter 10

Kamren laid across her parent's couch, with an aching back. Majority of the night, she tossed, and turned, worrying about Savage, Brody, and Big Head. Since she quietly entered her parent's house and didn't announce her presence, her mom was surprised to see her on the couch. It was 8:15 am, so Kamren had a lot of explaining to do.

Just as Kamren rolled over, Janice cleared her throat, with her arms folded across her breasts. Kamren's eyes open and she rolled over. She was startled to see her mom, but she said, "oh, hey, Mom, good morning. It is morning, right?"

"Yes, it's 8:17 am, but the better question is, when did you get here?" Janice questioned. Kamren yawned and rubbed her blurry eyes. Then she stretched a little and pulled the blanket off her body. Janet exhaled and sat down. Kamren was stalling, but she had enough time to get figure out why Kamren was here.

"I got here last night, but I didn't want to wake you guys."

"Kamren, why are you lying to me? I'm pretty sure you're here because you and Brody got into an argument." Janice said.

"You're wrong this time, Mom, Brody and I are good. Last night, Valerie and I went out for drinks. I thought I could drive home, but I couldn't. Since you guys stay closer, I knew it was smarter to come here instead."

"Kamren, you shouldn't be drinking and driving! You know better than that, why would you do that?" She asked.

"Mom, that's why I came here, but can you stop shouting? I have a headache and a hangover," Kamren rubbed her temples and closed her eyes. She had to make her mom believe her story and that she was suffering from a hangover.

"I'm sorry, baby, I'll get you some medicine and a Sprite." She smiled and said, rubbing Kamren's leg.

"Thanks, Mom," she smiled saying, but a knock on the door interrupted her. Janice and Kamren locked eyes, but Kamren stood to her feet saying, "I'll get that, Mom, it's probably Brody."

"Okay," she said, walking away. Kamren walked to the door hearing crying coming the door. Rushing to open it, Kamren found Valerie staring in jogging clothes and a face full of tears. Gasping, but covering her mouth, Kamren said, "Val, what the hell is wrong?" Without waiting for a response, Kamren hugged Valerie pulling into the house. The affection from Kamren didn't stop her crying, nor mend her pain.

"I'm sorry I came unannounced, but you were right from jump," Val flopped on the couch sobbing. Giving her mom a signal to not enter the living room, Kam sat next to Valerie asking, "V, what are you talking about?"

"I'm talking about Tyson, I caught him cheating on me this morning, Kam!! In our house, in my fucking bed!!"

"What, no, are you serious? You can't be serious!"

"Girl, I caught him cheating with some girl, I don't even know her. What I did find out is that she's friends with his sisters. I can't even think straight right now."

Chapter 11

Valerie stared at Savage as he watched television, but he ignored her for a special reason. He could tell she was jealous about who left his house a few minutes ago. She wanted answers, but he wasn't telling her anything. Since she claimed she didn't like him like that, it shouldn't matter who was at his house.

It's been four days since True Love was killed, but it felt like a life time. The last thing he needed right now was arguing, especially with a woman he was trying have relations with in the near future. Savage was grateful that Valerie was by his side in his time of need. It showed him that Valerie really cared, that was something he couldn't find in many people.

"Wasn't that the E.M.T. that was on the scene?" She asked.

"Yea, but why do you ask that?" Savage tried to stay serious, but he couldn't control the smirk that was written on his face.

"I asked, because I'm CURIOUS to know, now, answer my question!"

"If your nosy ass must know, yes, that was her. Her name is Karina Johnson and she's from Opelousas." He smiled.

"Why was her big booty here?" She snapped, but Savage laughed.

"You know what's crazy? You don't want me, but I can see it in your beautiful eyes that you're jealous. It's kind of cute though, I can't lie," Savage smiled. Valerie couldn't control the way he made her smile. She flipped him her middle finger and said, "I'm not jealous, I asked you a question. Seems like you're dancing around that, so I'll just leave," Valerie grabbed her purse and jumped to her feet. As she headed for the door, Savage laughed louder and chased behind Valerie. She didn't think it was funny how he dangled her feelings right in front her face.

"Girl, stop playing with me, and sit your ass down. You know if you leave, my lil' feelings will be hurt." Rolling her eyes again, but also exhaling, Valerie sat on the couch, giving Savage a kiss on the lips. At first, she wanted to play hard to get, but the more time she spent with Savage, Valerie couldn't do that anymore.

"Anyways, have you spoken to Rachel today?" Valerie asked.

"No, I haven't, but I called her twice. I guess she's sleeping or busy, but I'm sure she's going to call me back."

"Oh, okay."

As Savage reached for the remote controller, a knock on the door made him nervous. He wanted to reach for his iron, but he didn't want to make Valerie scared.

"Who is it?" Valerie asked.

"It's Kam."

"Damn it," Valerie whispered, but Savage began to laugh. He pointed to the door saying, "Open it." Valerie walked to the door opening it saying, "hey, girl, what's up?" Valerie stood at the door feeling like she was caught doing something wrong. Kamren sized her up and down looking confused, but walked in the house, closing the door.

"Uuuhhhh, I was coming to check on B, but looks like I found more than that. You and Brandon, since the fuck when?" Kamren snickered, whispering.

"Baby, I'll be right back so you two can talk. Thanks for coming to check on me, Kam."

"No problem, you know I'm always here for you," Kamren smiled while Savage walked away, entering his room, and closing the door. Before Kamren could say anything, Valerie covered her face, blushing.

"Okay, baby, what's going on, with you two?"

"I don't know, Kam, it's like we both need each other right now. I can't lie though, these past four days have been amazing with him. It's like I'm getting to know Brandon, and not Savage, he's a good guy."

"He is, but this is crazy, man. I guess you wanted some more of that dick," she whispered, laughing.

"Girl, fuck you," she giggled.

"Now that I see Savage is in good hands, I'm out. Tell him to text me later."

"Okay, I'll call you when I get to work," Valerie replied.

"Bet, bye." Valerie and Kamren stood to their feet walking to the door. Before walking out, Kamren turned around giving Valerie a hug saying, "do you see how God works?"

"Yea, I do now."

"Take care of him, okay?" Kamren said walking off.

"You know I will, but bye, for real, this time," Valerie laughed, closing the door. Savage then walked out of the room saying, "where did Kam go?"

"I guess home, she saw you were in good hands," she smiled, walking close to him. Savage pulled her in by the waist giving her a tight hug. If things continue to be like this between them, Valerie knew she would be in love in a matter of weeks.

"Real talk, I'm glad you're here with me, thanks for everything."

"I like being here," she smiled, wrapping his hands tighter around her waist.

"I wish you could stay here all day, but I know money calls you have to answer it.

"Do you need anything before I go to work?" Valerie asked.

"No, I'm good, have a good day at work," he kissed her lips saying.

"I'll try, bye," Valerie walked out of the door rushing to her car. Rain came out of nowhere drenching her clothing.

Grabbing the remote before sitting down, Savage flipped through the channels searching for the news station. Once he found what he was looking for, he didn't like what his eyes were seeing. With praise hands at his face pressed against his thin lips, Savage felt his body becoming cold. A destroyed look was on his face and there was nothing he could do to wipe it away. What he was watching on the news had his head aching and his palms sweating. He reached for his phone to call Brody, but his phone fell to the floor. He couldn't take his eyes off the television, but he wished he could. A dead body was found under the Huey P Long in Baton Rouge, Louisiana. Authorities said it was a female victim, but they weren't releasing any names yet. He had a gut feeling it was Rachel, because he hadn't spoken to her in two days. He checked her social media accounts, but none of them had recent posts.

"What the fuck is really going in this world?" He uttered to himself.

Savage still had Rachel's mom's number programmed in his phone, but he wasn't sure if he wanted to call her. He didn't want to ask her a bunch of questions, but he also didn't want to worry her with what he saw on the news. After debating with himself for three minutes, be built the courage to dial her number. On the second ring, she answered, but a lot of commotion took place in the background. He could hear her voice, but he wasn't sure if she said hello, so he increased the volume on his phone and asked, "hello, Mrs. Whitney, are you there?"

"Brandon, where are you?" She asked.

"I'm home, but where are you?"

"I'm at home, as well, can you come over? It's urgent and I need to speak to you." She shouted. Savage pulled the phone from his ear and rubbed the outer area of his ear.

"Yea, I can, but what's wrong?" He questioned.

"She's dead, Brandon, Rachel is dead!!"

"No, no, this can't be what I'm seeing on the news. Mrs. Whitney, are you sure???"

"I'm sure, Brandon, just please come as soon as you can," she ended the call without giving Savage a chance to respond. With trembling hands and more tears falling down his eyes, Brandon dropped the phone on the floor. His body wanted to move, but his heart prohibited that from happening.

The End

CPSIA information can be obtained
at www.ICGtesting.com
Printed in the USA
LVHW050046211218
601231LV00017B/394/P